THE MYSTERY OF MATTHEW GOLD

What do you do when the words won't come?

Chick Yuill

First published in Great Britain in 2019

Instant Apostle
The Barn
1 Watford House Lane
Watford
Herts
WD17 1BJ

British Library Cataloguing-in-Publication Data

A catalogue record for this book is available from the British Library.

This book and all other Instant Apostle books are available from Instant Apostle:

Website: www.instantapostle.com

E-mail: info@instantapostle.com

ISBN 978-1-912726-12-7

Printed in Great Britain.

contents

… that blessed mood,
In which the burthen of the mystery,
In which the heavy and the weary weight
Of all this unintelligible world,
Is lightened:
Lines composed a few miles above Tintern Abbey
William Wordsworth

… great is the mystery…
The First Letter of Paul to Timothy (AV)
Chapter 3 verse 16

mind-forged

2017

snapshot of a lonely man

chapter 1
2017

Matthew Gold woke with a start at four o'clock on the morning of the 11th March. His body was bathed in a cold sweat and his heart was beating rapidly.

There were three pages missing. The last three pages. The pages that made sense of the story. The pages where all the questions were answered and the mystery was solved. The pages that tidied things up, brought everything to a satisfactory conclusion. Even worse, try as he might, he couldn't for the life of him remember a sentence or even a single word that was on those missing pages.

He fumbled for the switch on the bedside lamp, pushed the duvet aside and sat up slowly on the edge of the bed, shivering and cursing the nightmare that had disturbed his rest yet again. He'd had that same dream so many times over the last twenty years. And every time it left him with a knot in his stomach that meant there would be no more sleep that night.

He half-sighed and half-moaned, a mix of irritation and resignation, as he struggled into his dressing gown and headed downstairs to the kitchen to make himself a cup of tea. At least the house was warm. His house was *always* warm. The darkness and chill of the long winter nights had troubled him since childhood, and he did everything he could to protect himself against the rigours of the British weather. It was a relief to him that these days his money allowed him to escape the cold, and he made sure that he took a couple of breaks and headed somewhere south to sunnier and warmer climes at this time of year.

He stood, leaning on the solid oak worktop of the island that sat in the middle of his expensively built but tastefully understated kitchen, and waited for the kettle to boil. The simple functional lines of the Shaker-style units, discreetly illuminated by the carefully recessed and perfectly positioned lighting, satisfied his lifelong desire for well-defined form and a clear sense of order. And the array of integrated, top-of-the-range appliances answered his need, bordering on obsession, for everything to be finished to perfection.

He allowed the kettle to go off the boil and stand for exactly seven seconds before pouring the water over the loose Earl Grey tea that he'd carefully measured into the porcelain teapot decorated with an embossed butterfly pattern. After half a minute, he stirred the contents of the pot, replacing the lid precisely so as to make as little noise as possible. A further thirty seconds passed before it was time to pour the tea into the cup. And the final act in this well-rehearsed ceremony was to cut a narrow wedge from a lemon that he took from the otherwise empty stainless-steel free-standing fridge and let it slip gently from his fingers into the tea. Only then did he allow himself the pleasure of putting the cup to his lips and taking the first sip. It was the culmination of a ritual he had practised several times a day for nearly forty years.

He prided himself in always making the perfect cup of tea at any time of day or night. In truth, despite the £50,000 he'd spent in having the kitchen designed and fitted, making tea was just about the extent of his cooking skills. He'd never actually made a proper meal in his life. Every gadget and every utensil, apart from the kettle, toaster and microwave, was in pristine condition simply because it had hardly ever been used.

If anyone else had been admitted to this sanctuary, they would surely have thought it odd that a man who knew nothing of the culinary arts had invested so extravagantly in a custom-built kitchen that would have been the envy of a professional chef. But, apart from the occasional repair man who answered Matthew Gold's call to put some piece of domestic equipment right, nobody had ever been admitted to the kitchen. Or, indeed, to any other part of his home. His neighbours knew little of the owner of what a local estate agent's brochure had gushingly described as 'an immaculately presented six-bedroom house nestling at the end of a private no through road in one of Wilmound's most exclusive and desirable neighbourhoods'.

In the nearly two decades he'd lived there he'd never exchanged more than a cursory greeting with anyone as he took his regular evening walk to the restaurant in the town centre where he always ate dinner at a table reserved for him in the corner by the window. Once, when there had been a power cut that had left the entire street in darkness for four or five hours, a well-meaning resident had called to ask if he was alright. The curt nod of the head and the seemingly ungrateful manner with which their enquiry was greeted was enough to ensure that no one ever called on him again. On the rare occasions when he would figure in their conversations, the common consensus was that 'the man's a mystery'. And that was just as he wanted it to be. He'd no need to be understood or accepted by others. He'd learned how to be alone. Loneliness, he'd discovered through long experience, was something that could be suppressed. To give into it would be weakness and would leave him vulnerable. And that was a mistake he was determined never to make again.

He sipped slowly from his bone china cup, savouring the aroma of the bergamot oil that gave his tea its distinctive flavour and that always conjured up in him a longing for warmer climes and sunnier days. He might have sat like this for another hour thinking of nothing in particular, had he not glanced at the clock on the wall opposite him. Its glowing red digital lettering told him not only that the time was 5.15, but also that the date was 11.03.17. *The 11th of March! His 70th birthday*. Matthew Gold was not a man who was given either to celebrating anniversaries or reminiscing on the past. He saw little point in looking back to less comfortable times. But in the quietness of the early morning he couldn't help but reflect on what a cold start to life it had been and how far he'd come. Or what a strange and sometimes unpleasant journey it had turned out to be.

tongue-tied

1947–1959

glimpses of a difficult childhood

chapter 2

1947

The vicious winter that rampaged across England in the first couple of months of 1947 encamped itself south of the border until the second week of March before ruthlessly invading the west of Scotland and dumping the heaviest fall of snow that anyone alive could remember. The Lanarkshire coal-mining town of Bellmill was right in the firing line. The occupants of the long parallel lines of back-to-back, single-storey, two-roomed miners' houses – known to everyone locally as 'the rows' – felt the full force of the blast. The gas lighting, which provided inadequate illumination at the best of times, flickered and faded completely as the temperature plummeted and the pipes that should have carried the gas froze. The coal fires that burned in the grates brought some warmth and strategically placed candles alleviated the gloom a little, but neither was a match for the cold draughts that rattled the doors and windows and penetrated into every part of the small brick-built dwellings.

It was in the house at the very end of the row and most exposed to the elements – 121 Pit Road – that, after a long and painful labour, Sarah Gold gave birth to her son at exactly three minutes past five on Tuesday morning 11th March. Her mother, Maggie, watched with arms folded and without betraying the slightest trace of emotion, as the midwife reached across the recessed 'hole-in-the-wall' bed that was separated only by a flimsy curtain from the rest of the room where the family lived their everyday lives. She lifted the tiny new-born baby and placed him gently in Sarah's arms. The young woman, who was barely seventeen years old, held her child for less than a minute. She had already stopped breathing when the midwife took the infant from her and laid him carefully beside his still and lifeless mother.

Ma Buchan, as she was known to generations of women in the town, had delivered hundreds of babies in her nearly forty years as a midwife. But she'd never got used to the sight of a woman, especially one as young and thin as this one, dying in childbirth. She wiped a tear from her eye with the back of her hand and turned to the woman who stood impassively behind her.

'Mrs Gold, yer wee lassie's gone. I'm so sorry. She didnae ha'e the strength to deal wi' such a hard labour. But she's left ye a bonnie grandson. He'll need a' the love and care ye can gi'e him.'

Maggie Gold appeared unmoved either by the scene she had just witnessed or by the midwife's expression of sympathy. The severity of her religious convictions was matched only by her certainty that for some reason God had chosen to place her below what should have been her proper station in life. She had concluded that the divine purpose in this seeming misalignment could only be so that her words and bearing should be a constant rebuke to her less spiritually enlightened neighbours. Consequently, her answer was delivered with a clipped precision and a careful avoidance of the Lanarkshire dialect, which she saw as just another symptom of the dire spiritual condition of those around her.

'It's for the best,' she said, her arms still folded and her face expressionless. 'It's the Lord's will. My daughter broke God's commandment and brought shame on her father and me. We must accept the fact that God has judged her unworthy of raising the child she has borne out of wedlock. We can only hope and pray that in her last moments she repented and found forgiveness for her lust and sin.'

Ma Buchan looked with disbelief at the woman who'd pronounced such a harsh judgement on her own daughter. Her first instinct was to say nothing, but she couldn't contain her indignation at what she'd just heard.

'Oh, Mrs Gold, she was only a wean hersel'. I'm no' religious like you an' I ken you're far wiser than me in these things. But I hope God will unnerstaun' the mistake yer daughter made an' take her intae heaven. Or He's no' a God I want to believe in.'

'What you or I want to believe in is beside the point,' Maggie Gold replied brusquely. 'God's ways are always just and right. He can't and won't turn a blind eye to wrongdoing, whatever excuses we try to make. Now I'll thank you to do what needs to be done here.'

It was plain to Ma Buchan that no purpose would be served by further discussion on either the sovereign righteousness of God or the sinful frailties of humanity, and she kept the rest of her thoughts to herself as she set about her work. She summoned a neighbour to attend to the child while she dealt with the laying out of the young woman's body with a quiet competence and a dignified sensitivity that came from years of living close to birth and death. Maggie Gold busied herself by bringing kettles from the tiny adjoining scullery and placing them on the hob over the fire to ensure an adequate supply of hot water.

Such was Matthew Gold's entry into the world. The tasks that had to be done absorbed the attention of the women in the room and there were neither tears to lament the life that had just ended nor smiles to celebrate the life that had just begun. Only the slowly breaking dawn acknowledged his birth. And its cold, grey light seemed only to presage the struggle that awaited him.

By the time Jimmy Gold arrived home just after seven o'clock, the midwife had gone and the house was silent. He pushed open the door that led straight from the street into the scullery where his wife was busy, just as she was every morning when he got home from working night shift in Number Three Pit. He looked at her questioningly. She said nothing, but shook her head and nodded towards the bed in the adjoining room where their daughter Sarah was lying under the 'laying out' sheet that every family in the street kept ready for those moments when death – a regular visitor in that time and place – had to be reckoned with. The short, stocky miner was no stranger to loss and bereavement, but the sight was enough to bring him to his knees. He half-staggered across the room, buried his head in the bed and shed bitter tears for the loss of his daughter.

He had been crying for several minutes when he became aware of his wife standing behind him. She made no physical contact with him and offered no words of solace.

'Now we've got to raise her bastard son,' she said.

Jimmy Gold turned his head slowly and caught sight of the rudimentary home-made crib that a sympathetic neighbour had brought on hearing of the birth and into which the midwife had placed the baby. In the wave of grief that had overwhelmed him he'd assumed that mother and child had died together. Now he pulled himself to his feet, a powerful resolution displacing the sense of desolation that had forced him to his knees. He walked the few paces across the room and lifted the baby out of his makeshift bed. To his wife's annoyance the coal dust on his clothes left black smudges on the sheet wrapped around the child. He ignored her protests.

'Aye, we've lost Sarah. If only she'd been able tae trust us and tell us sooner what had happened to her, we might ha'e been able to support her more. And she might ha'e been stronger. I think it was the shame that broke her heart.'

His wife was about to dispute his assessment of what had happened. But for once he would not be silenced.

'God knows, Maggie, I've gi'en intae you too often an' I've held ma tongue for the last twenty-five years just tryin' to keep the peace. But I'll ha'e ma say noo though it's too late to help Sarah. If you'd listened to the lassie rather than layin' down the law to her an' if I'd been stronger and more of a father tae her, then maybe she'd never ha'e ended up pregnant. But I promise ye, I'll make sure we take care of this boy and raise him right.'

Nothing more was said. Maggie Gold turned away and continued with her chores while he filled a large basin from the single cold tap and topped it up with warm water from the kettle that had been heating on the stove. Taking care not to spill a drop, he carried it out of the scullery and across the room where he set it down on the floor in front of the fire. Then he retraced his steps, closing the scullery door as he always did to ensure that his wife would not be offended by the sight of her husband washing. Only then did he strip off completely and wash himself vigorously as the tears continued to run down his face.

chapter 3
1951

Matthew Gold felt himself being hoisted onto Grampa's shoulders and carried through the crowd making their way from the old wooden stand at Murray Park. It was a familiar sensation he'd come to love. The five or six hundred people spilling out of the ground just before five o'clock on a Saturday afternoon were in high spirits, having witnessed Bellmill Rangers defeat their bitter local rivals to progress to the next round of the annual County Cup competition. But no one in that joyful procession of men was happier than the four-year-old boy who surveyed the scene from his vantage point above their heads. It wasn't the ninety minutes spent watching twenty-two men running up and down a football pitch that accounted for the pleasure he felt. His attention, as it always did, had started to wander shortly after the kick-off, allowing him to escape into the world of his vivid childhood imagination, only to return to reality in a burst of excited anticipation at the delights that always awaited him at the end of a match. The blast of the referee's whistle and the roar of the jubilant spectators signalled that the real fun of the afternoon was just beginning.

They made their way through the narrow side streets and back into the long, broad Main Street that ran through the town. The good-natured banter of the little group of men grew ever louder as they approached The Rabbie Burns, the pub to which they always headed to slake their thirsts after the hard work of offering their vociferous advice to the players who wore the claret and amber colours of the 'Gers. But Matthew knew that this would be one of the occasions when his grandfather would not be joining his pals at the bar. He also knew by heart how the conversation of the adults below him would go at this point.

'Ye'll no' be comin' in, Jimmy, I'm sure. It'll be on to the Tally's for you an' the wee fella?'

Tam Dornan always spoke for the group and Jimmy Gold always made the same reply.

'Aye, ye're right enough. Matty loves to go to Verricchia's, so it'll be a cup of tea for me today. But you boys enjoy your pint.'

That was the point at which the boy felt the sauntering steps of the man on whose shoulders he sat, now released from the restraints of ambling with his cronies, change to the broad, determined strides of someone with a mission in mind and no time to waste. Matthew put his arms round his grandfather's neck and held on tightly, his excitement growing with every step. It took less than five minutes to reach their destination, but for Matthew it seemed like an eternity before Grampa lifted him from his shoulders, high above his head, lowered him gently to the ground, and led him into the realm of mystery and magic that was revealed as they walked hand in hand through the ornate glass doors in front of which he'd just landed.

Verricchia's Ice Cream Parlour was the place he loved more than anywhere else on earth. Even before the dessert for which Mr Verricchia and his establishment were justly famous in the town arrived on the table, it was the ultimate sensory experience for a boy born into an age of post-war austerity and raised in a home where the matriarch regarded innocent pleasure and sin as interchangeable terms: the miracle of electric lighting, the secluded luxury of the booths with their dark-wood benches covered in plush red velvet cushions, the marble-topped tables that could cool sweaty hands in seconds, the sound of the gramophone in the corner playing the popular hits of the day that invited the listener to enter a different and more glamorous world. It was strange and wonderful and it conjured up within him longings that he could not put into words but that would stay with him for the rest of his life.

Matthew curled up with his legs tucked beneath him, watching and listening intently while his grampa went to the counter and ordered a pot of tea and a sandwich for himself and an 'ice cream sundae for my boy'. He liked it when Grampa called him 'my boy'. He was old enough to know that his mother had died and that Jimmy and Maggie Gold were his grandparents. But Grampa loomed so large in his life that it had never occurred to him that anything was missing or even to ask about his father. He was Grampa's boy and that was enough.

Mr Verricchia carried the tray to their table and chatted enthusiastically as he placed the items on the marble surface. His broken English, liberally sprinkled with Lanarkshire colloquialisms and delivered in his exotic-sounding Italian accent, fascinated Matthew, who assumed that their host came from a land of unbroken sunshine in which every room in every house looked just like the ice cream parlour. He thought that it must be a wonderful country in which to live and wondered why Mr Verricchia had left it to come to Bellmill. The good-natured proprietor ruffled his hair and invited his young customer to eat.

'Now sonny boy, I make the special ice cream for you. So enjoy.'

'And what do you say to Mr Verricchia?' Grampa asked, looking straight at him and pronouncing every word of his question slowly and deliberately.

Matthew took a deep, unhurried breath before he spoke, just as Grampa had taught him.

'Th-th-th-thank you, M-M-Mmmmister Vvverricchia.'

Grampa smiled approvingly and Mr Verricchia patted his head again.

'Well done, Matthew,' he said as he headed back behind the counter. 'Maybe one day I learn to speak English as good as you.'

What followed were moments of exquisite pleasure for Matthew. Getting his long spoon into the tall sundae glass was a task he performed with mixed success, but his childish efforts were a great source of amusement to them both. As usual he managed to get almost as much of its contents on to the table as in his mouth and Grampa made him laugh by suggesting that the random shapes formed by the spills looked like some people they knew. At times like this, Matthew's stammer almost disappeared and the conversation flowed back and forward between boy and man. Matthew wished that they could stay there forever. But all too soon he'd eaten his ice cream and Grampa's teapot was empty. They said goodbye to Mr Verricchia, went back through the enchanted doors by which they'd entered, and returned to the ordinary world they'd left just half an hour earlier.

They walked home slowly, neither of them wanting to arrive sooner than they needed to. As they crossed under the railway bridge and 'the rows' came into view, Matthew nodded his agreement at Grampa's reminder that, this being Saturday evening and Grandma having already begun to prepare her heart and mind for the disciplines and exercises of the Lord's Day tomorrow, it would be better that they didn't trouble her with the details of what they'd been doing. In fact, the advice was unnecessary. For the little boy knew in his heart, though he couldn't understand why it always happened, that his stammer would return with a paralysing intensity the minute they crossed the threshold of 121 Pit Road.

chapter 4
1953

The thirty members of Class Two at Bellmill Primary School were sorry when they were told that their regular teacher, Mrs Evans, was ill and wouldn't be in that day. They all liked Mrs Evans and Mrs Evans liked all of them. Their disappointment at the absence of their favourite teacher was all the greater when they learned that Mrs Evans' place would be taken by Miss Prinn who, as far as any of them could tell, didn't seem to like children at all. And even before the register for the day had been taken, their disappointment had already given way to a nervous fascination as they watched the scene playing out before them.

It had taken Miss Prinn only the briefest of glances on entering the classroom to spot something and someone that displeased her. And now she was growing ever more impatient with the pupil she'd immediately summoned to stand in front of her desk.

'Undo your scarf, boy – now! It's warm enough in school without all that clothing. Why, oh why, do mothers send their children to school looking like they're heading to the North Pole?'

Matthew Gold struggled to do as he was told, but it was proving to be an impossible task. His grandmother had sent him to school that morning with his thick brown woollen scarf criss-crossed over his body with both ends pinned together at the back. Try as he might, he couldn't make his five-year-old fingers, still numb from the cold outside, undo or even locate the safety pin that held the ends together behind his back. Miss Prinn's meagre store of patience was exhausted. She got up and strode from behind her desk.

'Here, I'll do it for you,' she muttered, shaking her head in despair and spinning the object of her ire around. 'And tell your mother not to dress you like that again.'

For the rest of his life he wished that he'd said nothing, just kept quiet and not tried to correct her mistake. But it was an instinctive reaction from a little boy who found it hard to understand why adults could get things so wrong and be so unkind at the same time.

'P-p-p-please, Mmmmmiss P-P-Prinn. It wwwas mmmy g-g-g-grandmother. Mmmy mmmother's d-d-d...'

He got no further with his sentence. Miss Prinn bent down until her face was only inches away from his. The veins in her nose stood out and her face became a shade of reddish-purple he'd never seen before.

'Don't be impudent, boy. What's your name?'

He was angry with himself when he realised that he was in a trap from which there was no escape. With the help of Grampa he'd learned to take deep breaths and get through most words and phrases eventually without it taking forever and without his stammer conquering him completely. But saying his name – saying it in front of lots of people, especially when he was nervous and anxious – was the thing he dreaded above everything else, the thing that could leave him powerless to utter a sound. Mrs Evans understood that. She would have been kind. She wouldn't have done this to him. But this wasn't Mrs Evans. This was Miss Prinn, who just kept staring at him and breathing the nasty smell of stale tobacco and mints into his face.

'Well, has the cat got your tongue, boy? Or are you Johnny No-Name? What's your name? We're not moving until you tell me.'

'M-m-m-m…' The more he tried to speak, the less sound that actually came out. He could see that Miss Prinn was willing to wait for as long as it took. His heart was starting to beat uncontrollably and his mouth was dry. It felt as if the whole world had stopped.

'Please, Miss Prinn, his name's Matthew Gold. He's got a stutter.'

Tommy Laird had a more developed sense of justice and a louder voice than most of his classmates and Matthew was relieved to hear him speak up on his behalf. At last it would all stop and he could go back to his place and sit down.

Miss Prinn, however, wasn't used to having her authority thwarted by a child, whatever impediment hindered him from obeying her instructions. This had become a battle of wills, one that she refused to lose.

'There you are then, Matthew Gold. We've helped you. One of your classmates has said your name and I've just repeated it for you. So now try again, a little harder. Let's hear you say it...'

Matthew tried to speak. He tried really hard. But something was happening to him. Something he couldn't quite understand. He felt sick and dizzy and hot and damp. He could hear someone call out, 'Miss, Matthew's wet himself,' and there was the sound of embarrassed giggling. After that he was only vaguely aware of losing his balance and slipping to the floor. He remembered nothing more until he woke up in the school nurse's office, waiting for his grandmother to come and take him home.

chapter 5
1955

Mrs Evans' class snaked their way slowly in single file behind their teacher into the school hall for the regular Friday Morning Assembly and took their usual places standing five rows from the front. Matthew Gold managed to position himself at the end of the row, as near as he could to the line of chairs arranged along the wall on which the teachers sat. He knew that Mrs Evans would be close enough to see and hear whatever was happening and that he'd be reasonably safe from Danny Johnstone. Danny was a head taller than any of his classmates and when necessary he used his height and strength to intimidate and torment anyone he thought was weak or vulnerable. But he rarely resorted to physical bullying, knowing from past experience that that kind of activity could quickly come to the attention of a teacher. It was much more effective and much more fun, he'd discovered, just to look out for someone who was a little different, someone with an unusual characteristic or disability, and humiliate them.

Matthew lived in almost constant fear of his unwanted attention. At any moment Danny's face would start to twitch and his breath would come in short bursts. One of his gang would immediately pick up the signal and ask the question that would launch the spiteful comedy routine that always reduced them to hysterical laughter. The enquiry would be made in a high-pitched voice that was intended to sound like Mrs Evans.

'And how are you today, Matthew?'

There would be a pause while Danny allowed the twitching to increase until his features began to distort. He'd learned to hold that pause until he could see the tears starting to well up in his unfortunate victim, who knew exactly what was coming next.

'Th-th-th-thank you Mmmmiss Eeeevans,' Danny would stammer. 'I'm g-g-g-good as G-G-G-Gold.'

Even his kinder classmates, who felt sorry for Matthew, but whose sympathy was outweighed by their fear of Danny and his pals, would join in the laughter. And Matthew would be left feeling utterly alone. There was little point in him trying to protest. His anger and confusion would simply make his stammer more acute, which only served to increase the derision. And reporting it to a teacher was definitely not an option. The worst sin in Bellmill Primary School was to be a *clipe*. It was a word from the local dialect that even the youngest child had learned and would utter as if they were spitting some foul-tasting liquid out of their mouth. The unwritten but unbreakable law of the playground made it clear that no crime was bad enough to warrant becoming a *clipe* and reporting the misdeed or its perpetrator to a teacher. So Matthew learned to say and do nothing other than to fight back the tears, walk away and push the pain down to somewhere deep in himself where he could pretend it didn't exist.

But Friday Morning Assembly was the highlight of the school week. It wasn't just that it was a safe place where he could be free from the attentions of Danny Johnstone for half an hour. What Matthew looked forward to most of all was that the whole school sang together. *Everybody sang.* Miss Prinn, who surveyed the ranks of the conscripted congregation from the corner of the stage, made sure that everyone was singing and that anyone whose mouth was not moving in time to the music, or from whom no sound seemed to be issuing, would face the full force of her considerable fury. It was the only time Matthew ever felt grateful for her presence.

Despite his previous unhappy encounter with her when he was in Class Two, Matthew was in no danger of incurring the wrath of Miss Prinn today. Unlike most of the boys, he never needed to be coerced into singing. He *liked* singing. Liked it because he liked music – any kind of music. Liked it because the flow of rhythm and melody allowed his words to come much more easily and naturally, especially in a song for which he'd learned the words by heart. Liked it because he could be the same as everyone else; he could join in and be part of the group. Just like he did at Murray Park when the men around him would sing about their footballing heroes, even though Grampa would tell him that some of the words weren't what little boys should be singing. That didn't matter to eight-year-old Matthew. It didn't matter because his fascination with words was even greater than his liking for music. He didn't have to know what the words meant.

Didn't have to know if they were nice words or the kind about which Grampa warned him, the kind of which his grandmother would disapprove – and there seemed to be such a lot of those – with an unsmiling look and a shake of her head.

He loved words. He loved everything about them; the shape of the letters when he wrote them down; the way they looked on the page; the sound they made when people said them aloud; the strange feeling they gave him when he repeated them to himself – a feeling of happiness and sadness and longing, all at the same time. It was an exquisite pleasure that made his frustration with his stammer all the greater. Grampa had told him about Eddie Banks, one of Bellmill Rangers' best players, whose leg had been broken in a car accident and who could never play football properly again. He imagined that when Eddie watched other people playing football, he must feel like he did when he heard other people saying words without any difficulty.

He would have gone on thinking about words had he not become aware that Mr Meldrum, the music teacher, was playing the last line of the tune as an introduction to the morning's hymn. There was a momentary pause before Miss Prinn began to conduct them in singing the first verse, the one they should all have memorised that week. Matthew sang and listened to those around him singing. And he allowed the words and the music to engulf him like a great silk cloth falling softly over him and covering him completely.

By cool Siloam's shady rill,
How fair the lily grows!

How sweet the breath, beneath the hill,
Of Sharon's dewy rose.

They were the most mysterious words Matthew had ever heard. He'd not the slightest idea who or what or where Siloam might be. And none of the teachers had bothered to try to explain the meaning of the poetry to their pupils. But that didn't matter to him. According to the hymn, Siloam was *cool*. And that made him think of the marble-topped tables in Mr Verricchia's Ice Cream Parlour, a place he loved. He'd never heard the word *rill* before, but if it was *shady*, then he imagined it must be a nice place to be on a hot day, especially if flowers like lilies and roses grew there. He tried to imagine what a *dewy* rose would look like. He glanced at Sharon, one of the girls in his class, and thought about *Sharon's dewy rose*. It wasn't surprising that she wasn't wearing a rose. It would have looked odd if she had been. The only time people did that, as far as he knew, was when they were going to a wedding. Not to school!

That's what words always did to him. They made him think of all kinds of unlikely things. But strangest and most wonderful of all to him was the line about *the breath, beneath the hill*. He'd puzzled all week over who was doing the breathing and how they managed to do it beneath a hill. Images of giants and weird figures he remembered from fables and fairy tales wandered in a long procession through his mind as he tried without any success to solve that puzzle. At least, he thought to himself, the breath of whatever creature it turned out to be was *sweet*. Not like Miss Prinn's breath that day she'd put her face close to his when he was in Class Two and all he could smell were stale cigarettes and mints.

The rest of the assembly went by without Matthew paying any attention to what was said. No one else in the hall noticed anything different about him as they filed out again and made their way to their classrooms. But something *was* different. And *someone* was different. An eight-year-old boy with a stammer that often locked him into a world of his own had passed through a door by which he'd only lingered previously. It was a door into a different and wonderful world. *The world of words.* He remembered Mrs Evans telling them when they'd done some painting that 'a picture is worth a thousand words'. Whether or not that was true he didn't know. What he did know was that he'd just discovered what for him would be a greater truth, one that would set the course of his life. One word, even one whose meaning he didn't know for sure, could create a thousand pictures.

chapter 6
1958

It had been raining heavily for two days and what should have been a grassy football pitch had become a quagmire that sucked the boots of the young footballers into its muddy embrace with every step they took. Grampa had come off night shift that morning and should have been fast asleep at home in bed. But this was a moment he wouldn't have missed for anything. He stood with the group of parents on the touchline, proudly watching his grandson make his debut for the football team after six years at Bellmill Primary School.

'I knew ye'd make it, wee man,' he'd told Matthew the day before. 'You're just one o' those boys that takes a wee bit longer to develop. Some o' the best fitba' players have been like that.'

Matthew had accepted the compliment with some embarrassment. He knew it meant a lot to Grampa and he didn't want to tell him that the only reason for his selection was that the two boys who would have been chosen to play on the right wing had both gone down with some kind of flu and had been off school for several days. He wasn't about to become overexcited about being picked for the team. And it wasn't just his painful awareness that he wasn't a very good football player that held his emotions in check. Although he quite liked football, he really hated mud and rain. If the prospect of turning out for his school team had failed to fill him with enthusiasm, the likelihood of having to run up and down on a cold, wet afternoon was even less appealing. And, as it turned out, the reality was as unpleasant as he had feared. The game was already well into the second half and he'd managed only one or two unproductive touches of the ball. He could hear the muttered derogatory comments from some of his teammates about his contribution to the game and he couldn't avoid the dark looks coming his way from the team captain, Danny Johnstone. At least, he thought to himself, it'll soon be full time and I can get showered, put on dry clothes and go home.

But football has a way of taking unexpected turns and throwing up unlikely heroes. With the score even at three goals each, Bellmill Primary was awarded a corner kick with only a few minutes remaining. Matthew trudged reluctantly forward to take his place with his teammates waiting for the ball to arrive in front of the goal. Whenever he tried to recall what happened next, it was always a blur in his mind. As best as he could remember, the wind caught the ball as it came off the head of Danny Johnstone, drifted over several better-positioned and more skilful players, landed in front of him and stuck in the mud just inches from the goal. Instinctively he poked out his right foot and somehow managed to make contact with the ball. To his amazement, it rolled slowly over the line and past the despairing reach of the goalkeeper. There was general rejoicing from the rest of the team. Danny Johnstone hugged him, even if he did call him 'a lucky…'. Matthew couldn't quite make out the last word in the melee that was swirling around him, but he suspected it wasn't entirely flattering.

When the final whistle went, Grampa was waiting for him on the touchline. Matthew had never seen him look more proud. He grabbed his grandson in his arms and hugged him tightly.

'Ye done great, wee man. Scorin' the winnin' goal, eh? I'm proud o' ye.'

'Wee man.' That was how he always addressed him when football was the topic of the conversation. Matthew didn't particularly like being called that, but he was too fond of Grampa to object.

'Thanks, G-G-Grampa. I think I was a b-b-bit llllucky. But I'd b-b-better g-go to the showers and then g-g-get changed. I'm getting' c-c-cauld.'

'Aye, right enough, son. I'll be waitin' for ye.' Then he added with a lift of his eyebrows, 'An' I think somebody else is waitin' for ye o'er there.'

Matthew glanced in the direction Grampa had indicated. He was surprised to see Elsie Brownlee standing on her own on the gravel path that led back to the main school building. She'd been watching the football match with a dozen other girls who'd all gone home by now. Elsie was in his class and was just a couple of months younger than he was, but they'd never really spoken to each other before. It wasn't his stammer that had kept him from talking to her in the past. A conversation with a *girl* was sure to be taken as an unmistakable sign that he was a 'cissy' and would have attracted the derision of every other eleven-year-old boy in the class. And a conversation with the girl now standing in front of him would never have escaped the attention of Danny Johnstone and his followers. Elsie had prominent teeth, curly ginger hair, and – the most distinctive and worst thing of all in a Lanarkshire school – she spoke with an *English* accent. He'd noticed that she sometimes smiled at him when they passed in the corridor, but he'd made a point of never smiling back at her.

'Hi, Matthew,' she said very quietly as he came level with her. 'Can I talk to you for a minute, please?'

He wasn't quite sure how to respond. But after quickly checking that none of the other boys were around to see them, he nodded and stood awkwardly in front of her, trying to avoid her gaze.

'I just wanted to say that I was really pleased you scored the winning goal today. I thought you played really well.'

Matthew was accustomed to feeling nervous and embarrassed and tongue-tied. But this was different. He wasn't used to unexpected compliments like this. And never from a girl. He might have stammered his thanks if he could have thought of what to say. All he managed to do was to nod his head and shuffle his feet. At the same time, he felt himself blushing uncontrollably. And that was followed immediately by a sudden panic as he tried to think what he should do next. He needn't have worried. Elsie hadn't finished what she wanted to say to him.

'And I think you're really good the way you just ignore Danny Johnstone and those boys. They sometimes call me "buck teeth" and "gingernut" and imitate my accent. My mum wanted to come and complain to the school, but I wouldn't let her. I told her about you, and how you don't let them get you down, and how I'm just trying to ignore them like you do. She said I should talk to you and see if we could help each other. I don't think she understands that boys and girls don't get together like that at school. Anyway, we're probably going back to England again with my dad's work.'

Matthew still didn't know what to say. He hadn't ever thought much about *other people* being called names and poked fun at, and it added to the confusion he was already feeling. It made him angry that Danny Johnstone seemed to be able to do just whatever he wanted. And he had an overwhelming feeling of sympathy for the girl who was talking to him. He'd assumed until then that girls just got on with being girls and didn't know what it was like to be bullied. But what took him by surprise was that Elsie's words made him feel less lonely. Somebody else knew what it was like to be on the receiving end, to be the butt of the jokes, to stand there fighting back the tears while everybody around you laughed. Maybe girls weren't as different as he'd imagined. But even as that thought passed through his mind there was something coming from somewhere else inside him telling him that they really were *very* different from boys.

Once again Elsie rescued him as he tried to work out what was happening to him.

'Thanks for letting me talk to you,' she said with a smile that threw him into even greater confusion. 'I know you don't want the other boys in the team to see you. And my dad will be worried if I'm late home.'

He wasn't sure if she really did touch him on the arm as she walked away or if he just imagined that. And though he loved words, he couldn't think of any that could describe what he was feeling. He might have stood there forever, not knowing what to do. But this time it was Grampa who rescued him from his inability to move or speak.

'I've been watchin' you from o'er there. Ye're a real fitba' player now. Fitba' players have always got lassies runnin' after them. But I think it's time you got showered. I'll be waitin' for you.'

He grinned at Grampa and headed for the changing rooms. He wasn't sure why he was feeling so pleased with himself. And then he remembered. He'd just scored the winning goal...

chapter 7
1959

It was a warm and sunny afternoon at the end of June. For Matthew and his classmates it was their last day at Bellmill Primary. Tomorrow the long break from school would begin and in another six weeks they'd be moving on to the next stage of their education at what everyone excitedly referred to as 'Big School' – Bellmill Academy. Their teacher, a former major in the British Army, and normally a stickler for discipline who insisted on his pupils working until the bell sounded, had allowed them to play board games since lunchtime as they waited to be summoned to the school hall for the Annual Prize-giving and a final pep talk from the headmistress.

Matthew had been delighted when his favourite teacher, Mrs Evans, had been appointed to the post twelve months earlier. Just as he'd hoped, she'd taken a firm line against any kind of bullying. As a consequence, his last year at the school had been largely trouble free and he'd been generally happier than at any time previously. As his sense of well-being increased, his stammer had eased a little and there had been a corresponding improvement in his schoolwork. He knew that when they assembled in the school hall in just half an hour, he was to be presented with the first prize in the Year Eight Essay Writing Competition. So, when the school secretary came to say, 'Mrs Evans would like to see Matthew Gold in her office, please,' he guessed that it was just to tell him what he should do when he went up to collect his award. As he walked along the corridor with the secretary, he thought to himself that Mrs Evans probably wanted to tell him that he wouldn't need to say anything. She was always kind like that and wouldn't want him to be worried about his stammer.

The secretary knocked on the door, pushed it open, and said, 'It's Matthew Gold, Mrs Evans.'

'Come in, Matthew, and take a seat,' she said, nodding to the secretary to close the door and leave them alone.

Matthew went to stand in front of her desk, but Mrs Evans signalled to him to take a seat on the big leather couch in the corner of her office. Then she sat down beside him and clasped her hands together. He wasn't sure why, but he suddenly began to feel nervous. Something wasn't right. Mrs Evans was speaking very gently.

'Matthew, I have to tell you some bad news. After you left for school this morning, your grandfather became ill and had to be taken to hospital...'

He could feel his heart beating and his mouth getting dry, just like it always did when he became anxious. He wanted to say, 'Is Grampa alright?' but the words wouldn't come out.

'I'm really sorry to tell you that we've just had a call from your grandmother at the hospital. He died just a little while ago.'

Matthew was used to having difficulty putting together the words he wanted to say. But this was worse. Worse than dealing with his stammer. Now he was having difficulty sorting out the words he was *hearing*. They didn't make sense. Why was Mrs Evans saying these things? What did the words 'your grandfather' and 'died' have to do with each other? For a moment it was as if nothing was real, as if he wasn't really there. He wasn't sure what was happening. It was like someone else was crying as the tears began to run down his face, making dark, wet patches as they fell on to his grey school trousers. The tears gave way to deep sobs and he instinctively reached out towards Mrs Evans. She must have held him in her arms for five minutes until he sat upright and wiped his eyes on his sleeve. He had to do something.

'I'm ssssorry, Mmmmrs Evans.' He could hear himself speaking loudly through his sobs. 'I c-c-c-can't wwwwait to get my prize. I n-n-n-need to see my grampa. I need to g-g-g-go to the hhhospital.'

'I understand, Matthew.' Mrs Evans patted him on the hand. 'We'll get one of the teachers to drive you. Your grandmother is waiting until you get there. And don't worry about your prize. I'll make sure that you get it.'

In Matthew's memory, a thick fog hung over everything else that happened that day: the drive to the hospital; being hugged by his grandmother – something that always made him feel uncomfortable; learning that Grampa had suffered a heart attack after he'd left for school that morning and had never regained consciousness; waiting in a queue for a bus to get back home from the hospital in the evening; being told he should eat something before going

46

to bed, though he felt sick at the thought of food; trying to sleep knowing he'd never see Grampa again. It made him think of when he was very young and Grampa would allow him to try on his reading glasses, just to see what things would look like. Everything would become hazy, distant, unfocused; colours and shapes merging into each other. It had been that kind of day. The only thing that stood out clearly was the one thing that *hadn't* happened. Despite his repeated pleas, his grandmother insisted that it wouldn't be good for him to see Grampa's body. That made him angry. He wanted to tell her that he loved his grampa more than she'd loved her husband. But he said nothing and bottled up his anger.

His anger only increased as the days passed. Grampa's funeral was at his grandmother's church, though she never referred to it in that way. She called it 'the Fellowship'. Matthew knew the word 'fellowship' meant something like being good friends or a happy family. But his grandmother's Fellowship never felt like that to him. Unlike the crowd at Murray Park, they didn't approve of singing or music. And unlike the crowd at Murray Park, they never seemed to believe that they were on the winning side or that there was anything to celebrate. The man who was leading the service spoke a lot about the certainty of death and the need to be prepared for it when it came. But, to Matthew's annoyance, no one mentioned what a kind man his grampa had been. Surely that was the kind of thing you'd talk about in a real Fellowship.

He couldn't quite admit it to himself, but he was even more angry at Grampa. Why did he have to die like that? Coming home from the night shift in the coal mine, sitting reading the paper and eating his breakfast, falling off his chair into a heap on the floor. No chance of saying goodbye. Why did he have to die when he was only fifty-two? It was stupid to die at that age, when he must have known how much his grandson needed and loved him. And the more he thought about it, the more his anger began to shift again. His grandmother often talked about God allowing people to live for 'threescore years and ten'. That added up to seventy years. So, if God was *just* – and that was what the man who was leading the service kept saying – then why would he steal eighteen years from Grampa? And that led him on to another question. What kind of God would give him a stammer and make it so difficult to get his words out and allow people like Danny Johnstone to laugh at him? That didn't make any sense.

There was only one conclusion he could reach. His grandmother and the people in the Fellowship were wrong. Either there wasn't any God or, if there was, He wasn't the kind you'd want to get to know. And if there were any answers to his questions, he'd have to find them out for himself.

chapter 8
1959

The second week of the long summer break had dragged by slowly for Matthew. The boy who lived three doors away, and with whom he sometimes spent time, had gone to stay with relatives in Edinburgh for a month, leaving Matthew at a loose end. He'd been to the library and taken out several books that he'd read quickly but without much interest. The truth was that it had been difficult for him to get interested in anything much since Grampa's funeral. And today he was alone in the house and wondering what he could do to pass the time. His grandmother had gone out for the afternoon to deliver some of her late husband's clothes to someone in the Fellowship who knew of an out-of-work father of three children living in the next town who would benefit from them.

On an impulse, he decided to look under the hole-in-the-wall bed, the bed in which his grandparents slept and in which he knew his mother had died. In a house like this, with very little storage space, all kinds of things were shoved there out of the way. He hoped he might find something that would alleviate the boredom of an afternoon with nothing else to do. Sliding aside the curtain that hung from the wooden base on which the mattress rested, he switched on the torch he'd taken from the cupboard where Grampa had kept it ready for emergencies, and peered into the dark space. All he could see were dusty cardboard boxes. The base was about eighteen inches from the floor, enough space for someone of his age and size to crawl under, so he decided to investigate more closely.

He pulled out the first few cardboard boxes and sat on the floor opening them. They were filled with blankets or clothes, nothing that would brighten his afternoon, and he quickly closed them again. But before he pushed them back into place, he flicked the torch on again and slid himself under the bed one more time. There had to be something more exciting than what he'd found. He wriggled his way past an old wireless, bumped his head on a broken stool that was lying on its side, and grazed his arm against what looked like part of an ancient sewing machine he could vaguely remember his grandmother using when he was just starting school. He was about to abandon his search and return to the daylight when the beam of his torch lit up a wooden chest that had been pushed tightly into the corner. It was the kind of object that would have made any boy of his age think of pirate treasure and long-hidden gold. Here, at last, was something that might make all his snake-like squirming worth the effort and discomfort. The chest was heavy and scraped against the bottom of the bed base as he tugged it towards himself. He thought that it must have been even more difficult to push it in than to pull it out. Someone had gone to considerable trouble to make sure it was out of reach and well hidden.

It was a good five minutes' work to drag it all the way to the edge of the bed and get it into the light where he could see it properly. He took his handkerchief out of his pocket and used it to wipe the dust off the chest. He liked what he could see. It was just like pictures he'd seen of the kind of trunks seafarers would take with them on their voyages to far-flung ports across the world. Two broad iron bands, held by brass studs, ran down the front and back and over the rounded lid. On either side it had strong leather handles and it was clasped firmly shut by a large brass lock.

Matthew gazed at it for several minutes, wondering what could be inside and how he might get it open. He went to the drawer in the sideboard where the keys for all sorts of things were kept and rummaged through it, but he couldn't find anything that looked the right size or shape to fit the lock on the chest. Then he remembered that whenever they got home from Murray Park, Grampa would wait for the right moment when his wife was in the kitchen and pull out an old tobacco tin from a crack in the brickwork between the fireplace and the wall. He'd take some things from his pocket, put them into the tin, and return it quickly and quietly to its hiding place. He'd wink at his grandson, tap his nose with his forefinger and whisper, 'That's our wee secret.' Matthew, who knew how much Maggie Gold disapproved of smoking or gambling of any kind, had always assumed that it was where he kept his tobacco or the little slips he brought from the betting shop when he'd had a flutter on the horse racing. Now it occurred to him that the chest he'd just discovered might be another of Grampa's secrets and that it might be linked to the tobacco tin in some way.

He went across the room, put his hand into the gap in the wall behind the fireplace and fumbled for the tin. It was still there! He drew it out slowly and carefully. It gave him a strange feeling to think that he was the first person – the only person – to handle it since Grampa had tucked it away for the last time. He eased off the lid and examined the contents. There were a couple of old betting slips sitting on the top, just as he'd suspected there might be, and underneath the betting slips was a crisp £5 note. Grampa must have had a lucky win recently. As he took hold of the money and the pieces of paper and laid them on the floor beside him, his fingers felt something else on the bottom of the tin, something hard with ridged edges. *It was a brass key*. He picked it up carefully and dropped it into his pocket before putting everything else back in the tin and slipping it back into the hole in the wall. He glanced at the clock on the mantlepiece and saw that it was twenty to three. His grandmother had told him to expect her home around three o'clock. That gave him twenty minutes. Long enough to open the chest – provided this was the right key – see what was inside, lock it up again, slide everything back under the bed and draw the curtain that hung from the base. No one would be any the wiser.

His hands trembled slightly as he eased the key into the lock and turned it gently. The mechanism yielded immediately to his pressure and the clasp sprung open. He was about to push the lid up when he had a sudden unwelcome thought. Just before the end of term, Danny

Johnstone had created a stir among the other boys in the class when he'd brought some magazines to school. He'd charged his eager audience sixpence each for the chance to flick through the pages for themselves and examine the photographs closely. But first he'd been careful to warn them not to leave any marks or grubby fingerprints. He needed to be able to put them back where he'd found them, he explained, without his dad noticing that they'd been missing. What if Grampa had been like Danny's dad? What if this was where he'd kept *his* secret hoard of dirty magazines? Matthew didn't want to think of Grampa like that and for a moment he considered just locking the chest again and pushing it back into the darkness under the bed. But his curiosity was stronger than his embarrassed concern and he slowly lifted the lid, still nervous about what he might discover inside.

To his relief, what he found seemed innocent enough compared with Danny's dad's magazines. The chest was half-filled with books – there must have been at least fifty of them – both hardbacks and paperbacks. He glanced at the titles and the names of the authors. But, apart from two Sherlock Holmes stories, which they'd read at school, there was nothing with which he was in any way familiar. What he did recognise on the title page of each book he opened, however, was the name JAMES GOLD written in Grampa's handwriting. And in each book, underneath his name, again in his grampa's script, were two dates: the first, when he'd started reading the book; and the second, when he'd finished it. Matthew was puzzled. Grampa had often encouraged him with his reading. But, as far as he could tell, the only thing Grampa ever read was the newspaper. He would have loved to have talked to him about books. Why hadn't he ever said anything?

The answer to that question came sooner than Matthew could have imagined. He heard the front door open and before he could close the lid and slide the chest back under the bed, Maggie Gold was standing in front of him. It was only ten to three. She'd come home early.

'What on earth do you think you're doing?' she demanded angrily.

'I'm not d-d-d-doin' anything,' Matthew replied, not quite truthfully. 'I was j-j-just l-l-looking for sssomething.'

It made him angry with himself that his stammer always got worse when his grandmother asked him a question.

'Well, you can stop looking. And where did you find that trunk?'

'It was... it was... under the b-b-bed. It's f-f-full of b-b-books wwwith Grampa's nnname in them.'

'So that's where he hid them.'

She shook her head and sniffed in a way that left Matthew in no doubt that her disgust at what she was looking at far outweighed any grief she might have felt for the loss of her husband.

'B-b-but they're n-n-not dirty books! Not like Danny's dad's,' he blurted out.

'I should think not! Not in this house. Though they're not much better. I warned him never to let you see them. Cheap mysteries and detective stories. In all the years we were married he never once tried to better himself. Football and trashy books. That was him. I don't think he ever

54

thought deeply about anything. He was a disappointment to me.'

She almost spat the words out of her mouth and Matthew stared at her, angry and amazed at her unexpected outburst. He knew there had never been much warmth in his grandparents' relationship, certainly on his grandmother's part. But the contempt with which she spoke of his grampa left him shaken. He fought back the tears. He'd never liked his grandmother but he'd never felt a hatred for her like he did in that moment.

Maggie Gold was speaking again, more quietly than before. Matthew sensed that she was regretting her words. But she offered no apology.

'Put all that stuff back where you found it and we'll say no more about it. Just make sure I don't ever have to look at it again.'

Matthew did as he was told. He closed and locked the chest, pushed it back under the bed, and slipped the key into his pocket, unseen by his grandmother, who turned away and busied herself in the scullery. Nothing else was said between them that day. But they both knew something had happened that could never be undone. A festering sore that had been partially hidden but would never be healed had been exposed. For the next few years, to enable them to coexist under the same roof, they would try to cover it over with a dressing of perfunctory conversation and polite distance. But in that moment, they both knew it was a wound that would prove fatal to their relationship.

Meanwhile, the middle-aged woman retreated into the security of her unassailable convictions, and her twelve-year-old grandson made two resolutions: he would read every one of the books he'd found in the chest under the bed and he would leave home as soon as he was old enough.

headstrong

1959–1966

pictures of an angry young man

chapter 9
1959

Matthew Gold was uncomfortable and unhappy. He was ready to leave home for his first day at Bellmill Academy wearing his school uniform, which had been bought second-hand at the school shop. He hated that stupid uniform. It was bad enough that his blazer was worn at the elbows, though after trying it on half a dozen times, he'd worked out that if he stood with his arms in what admittedly was an unnatural position, there was just a chance that people might not notice the threadbare material. What was much more embarrassing and impossible to hide was that it was a couple of sizes too large. He'd 'grow into it', his grandmother had insisted. That would allow him to get a couple of years' wear out of it and save money. He was tempted to run away and hide somewhere where nobody would be able to see him. But he knew what had to be done. And he knew he couldn't put it off any longer.

Maggie Gold paused from her usual morning routine of household chores as her grandson grabbed hold of his school bag and headed towards the door. He could still remember her kissing him when he left for his first morning at primary school as a five-year-old, and for one terrible moment he was afraid that she might feel she ought to do it again. To his relief, she wiped her hands on her apron, took a step back and looked at him.

'Well, at least you've got the opportunity to make something of yourself,' she said matter-of-factly. 'Just make sure you take it. Don't end up like your grandfather. You shouldn't have to spend *your* working life digging coal underground and die an early death, leaving your wife and family to fend for themselves.'

He wanted to tell her that he hated her, that he wished she'd been the one who'd died. But he kept his thoughts to himself, mumbled something about not wanting to be late, and hurried out of the door. It was less than two months since Grampa had died. How could she even *think* something like that? And how could she *be* like she was? The summer had been unusually warm, but the atmosphere at 121 Pit Road had remained frosty and communication between them had been terse and tense. Since Grampa had died, they hadn't spoken a word more than was necessary to allow them to coexist under the same roof.

Fortunately, the long light days had allowed him to spend hours out of doors on his own. And he'd spent the time well. After his grandmother had discovered him with the chest half-full of Grampa's books, he'd feared that she'd want to get rid of it immediately. But that never happened, and he began to think that, for some reason, she was reluctant even to touch the chest or its contents. She never referred to it again and he guessed that all she wanted was for it to be out of sight and out of mind. He knew exactly what he would do. He waited until she'd gone out one afternoon, pulled the old chest out again and took a pile of books, which he hid in his room. By the time his grandmother got back, the chest was back in place and he had everything he needed to begin to keep one of the promises he'd made to himself. He'd start reading Grampa's books and give himself something to do for the rest of the school holiday.

Every morning he'd make the excuse that he was going to meet a friend and leave as early as he could with some sandwiches and a bottle of water tucked into his satchel for his lunch. But secreted in with the sandwiches there would always be one of Grampa's detective stories. All through those long summer days he would sit under the shadow of one of the old coal tips that surrounded the town and engross himself in tales of murder and mystery. Over the course of a few weeks, he came to know and love as unusual a group of companions as any twelve-year-old boy had ever met. He read avidly and uncritically, not pausing too long with words he hadn't previously come across or worrying unduly about situations he didn't fully understand. It was like being welcomed into the company of adults – but really *interesting* adults – who accepted him as an equal and invited him just to listen and learn. For the first time in his life there were hours at a time when he would completely forget his stupid stammer and the feeling of isolation that went with it. He was happy to be in the company of the cleverest and most articulate friends he could wish for – people he liked and wanted to *be* like, people who could find out answers and solve mysteries.

So, as he headed for school that morning, he walked in step with a small procession of elite detectives whose appearance would have amazed the townspeople of Bellmill had they been able to catch a glimpse of what he could see clearly in his mind's eye. There was a round-faced little man, no taller than Matthew himself, dressed in a priest's cassock, carrying a shabby black umbrella, and wearing a black felt hat with a low crown and a wide brim. Beside him walked an impeccably dressed but even shorter individual with an egg-shaped head perched a little to one side, a precisely trimmed moustache, and a pink-tipped nose. But if these two, with their short legs, had to hurry to keep up with a boy on his way to his first morning at secondary school, a third man sauntered along lazily with the languid air of a member of the British aristocracy – which is exactly what he was. Strolling alongside Father Brown and Hercule Poirot in his imagination, was Lord Peter Wimsey, his straw-coloured hair hanging loosely under his top hat and his long, narrow face with its supercilious expression made all the more absurd by the monocle that enabled him to 'take a squint' at anything requiring his close attention.

Even these three famed practitioners of the art of the private detective, however, were in awe of the fourth member of their quartet who was striding out ahead of them that morning. Tall and lean, his sharp, piercing eyes, hawk-like nose and prominent chin identified him immediately as the doyen of the detective fraternity, the resident of 221B Baker Street himself – Mr Sherlock Holmes. The people who passed on the street that morning saw nothing and no one other than an awkward schoolboy in an ill-fitting blazer. But long days of uninterrupted reading and a speech impediment that drove him back on his own company had made them as real to Matthew Gold as the people who lived next door.

Almost before he realised it, he'd reached his destination and was bidding farewell to his four imaginary acquaintances and walking slowly and nervously through the gates of his new school. Its intimidating appearance belied its more mundane objectives. Despite its impressive title and imposing buildings that wouldn't have looked out of place fronting the campus of a medium-sized university, Bellmill Academy had no pretensions to be an elite centre of learning. It unsentimentally disgorged the majority of its pupils at the age of fifteen, having efficiently discharged its primary responsibility to provide them with sufficient education to equip them to be decent citizens and enable them to find lifelong employment in the town's large steelworks, in one of the nearby coal mines, or in any number of local shops and small factories.

Matthew, however, was among the 20 per cent of its annual intake who, having successfully negotiated the entrance exam, were given the opportunity to pursue a more academic curriculum that it was hoped would fit them for a place at one of Scotland's universities. So, while most of his former classmates at primary school headed left for the main hall once they had entered the Academy grounds, he turned right towards a smaller building that housed the 'Higher Grade' section and joined the group of around fifty equally nervous twelve-year-olds standing and waiting apprehensively in an otherwise empty and echoey hall for whatever was supposed to happen next.

They didn't have long to wait. An elderly white-haired man wearing a dark suit and a black academic gown entered from a side door and mounted a small raised dais. He identified himself as the deputy headmaster, read out two lists of names, assigned everyone to either class 1A or 1B, directed them to the appropriate rooms, and walked out again without a further word.

Matthew followed the other twenty-three pupils who would make up 1B and found a space near the back of the room at a double desk, with no one sitting next to him. That would be a good place to avoid being noticed. He didn't want to be asked to say his name on his very first day with a bunch of kids he didn't know. His plan was about to be foiled.

'Good morning, 1B. Time for you to sit up and listen up.'

The voice boomed out even before the speaker came striding through the open door, his gown swishing behind him.

'I'm Mr McFadyen and I'll be your English teacher this year.'

The man standing in front of class 1B had an unruly mop of slightly greying hair that seemed to stick out in every direction in a series of random spikes and tufts. It looked to Matthew as if he'd tried, without much success, to cut it himself. His beard, which had a contrasting ginger hue, gave the appearance of having been hacked, equally unsuccessfully, with the same pair of blunt scissors he'd used on his head. He placed the pile of papers he was carrying under his arm on his desk and stroked his chin with his right hand as he scrutinised the faces in front of him. Twenty-four pairs of eyes stared back at him, uncertain as to what he might say or do next, or how they should react.

'I've also been assigned the onerous but gratifying task of looking after all you ladies and gentlemen during your first year. Soooo…' He stretched out the word for several seconds before continuing. 'We're going to get to know each other *very* well. I will always address you by your proper titles, in a fittingly formal manner. But you can all call me by my first name.'

As he delivered that last sentence, he spread his arms wide to emphasise that this was a privilege accorded to everyone in the room. Then he slowly folded his arms, leaned forward, and added in the conspiratorial tones of someone admitting a few chosen friends to a secret society from which the rest of the world was excluded:

'My first name is… Sir!'

His youthful audience was too mesmerised by his striking appearance and his sonorous voice to get the joke or to respond with the laughter he'd anticipated. Undeterred by their silence, he broke into a deep, rumbling chuckle and perched himself on the edge of his table, spilling the papers he'd laid there a moment before. A girl sitting in the front row stood up and went to pick them up for him.

'Oh, don't trouble about those.' He chuckled again. 'I'll get those later. We've got more important things to do for the next forty minutes. I want to find out what you've all been up to over the holidays. Let's see how many of you we can fit in before the bell goes for the end of this period.'

He pulled a sheet of paper from the inside pocket of his jacket, held it up with a theatrical flourish and slowly unfolded it.

'Now then, now then... I've got all your names here. Let's start with Mr Anderson – Mr Thomas Anderson. Then we'll hear from Miss Susan Bell. Tell us all what you've been reading for the last few weeks.'

He addressed the same question to a number of his pupils, drawing answers that ranged from popular weekly comics and football annuals to classic children's books. By the time a response had been solicited from Mr Ian Fraser, Matthew was in a state of panic. *Mr McFadyen was working alphabetically through his list. Gold would probably be next.* He'd have to speak in front of people he didn't know. He heard the words he'd been dreading coming from the front of the classroom.

'Now, where is Mr Matthew Gold?'

The room seemed to have gone very quiet and he could hear his heart beating as he raised his hand to identify himself.

'Aah... Mr Gold is on the back row. Not the best place from which to address your new colleagues who want to see you and get to know you. Stand up and speak up, Mr Gold. Everyone else, swivel yourself around so you can see Mr Gold as he addresses us.'

Matthew's face was getting hotter and redder as he got to his feet. The last vestiges of confidence drained from him as he realised everyone was looking directly at him. He tried to take deep, slow breaths but the words were taking a long time to come.

'Sssir, I've… I've… b-b-been rrreading sssome d-d-detective stories…'

He could hear the sound of sniggering from the far corner of the room where a group of boys were sitting together. Somebody was whispering something. He couldn't make out what they were saying, but it had the effect of increasing the laughter. He was fighting back the tears that were welling up. He lowered his head and stared at the floor, overcome with shame and despair. It was going to start all over again – the taunting and the mimicking – and it would be ten times worse than at primary school. For the second time that day he wished he could just run away and hide. He felt a firm hand on his shoulder and looked up to see that Mr McFadyen was standing next to him.

'Thank you, Mr Gold.' His voice sounded reassuring. 'Please resume your seat for a moment while I say something to the members of class 1B.'

Matthew sat down, grateful to have been rescued from a situation from which he'd seen no escape and relieved that everyone's attention was now turned away from him and fixed on Mr McFadyen, who'd walked back to the front of the room. He spoke very softly but with a precision that made sure every word could be clearly heard by everyone in the room. The jovial manner in which he'd greeted them had given way to a carefully controlled anger that none of his hearers would easily forget.

'Whenever you are in my classroom – indeed, wherever you are in this school – you will treat everyone with respect. *Everyone.*' He paused to allow that word to sink in. 'When anyone speaks, we accord them the courtesy of listening to every word they say. And we *never* interrupt. That applies whether it is a teacher, a member of the school staff, or another pupil. Any failure to observe that standard of conduct will be treated severely by me. Now… does everyone understand?'

His question was greeted with a stunned silence. His eyes narrowed as he repeated it more slowly and with added emphasis.

'DO YOU UNDERSTAND?'

He'd entered the room half an hour earlier like a jester intent on amusing his audience. Now he had the air of a judge demanding an answer from a guilty and evasive prisoner. No one needed to be prompted a second time. With one voice twenty-four twelve-year-olds assured him that his words were indeed understood and would be acted upon. Immediately his previous good humour reasserted itself and the atmosphere in the room relaxed.

'Now, ladies and gentlemen,' he said, lifting himself into a sitting position on the table and allowing his legs to swing loosely in front of him, 'we will give our total attention to Mr Gold. And, Mr Gold, don't stay hidden away on the back row. Please come to the front of the room and sit on the table beside me. And feel free to take your time. We've still got ten minutes before the end of this period. And I'm pretty sure you've got something interesting to tell us. What was it? Oh yes, you've been reading detective stories. Tell us more.'

And so for precisely nine minutes and twenty-six seconds – the longest he'd ever spoken to a group of people in his entire life – Matthew Gold addressed class 1B, sitting on the edge of the teacher's table at the front of the room, dangling his legs just like Mr McFadyen was doing. He told them – slowly, hesitatingly, and not without a fair amount of stammering – about his discovery of the writings of G K Chesterton and Agatha Christie and Dorothy L Sayers and Sir Arthur Conan Doyle. And he told them why he liked detective stories that were all about finding answers and solving mysteries. He didn't tell them about Grampa or his sudden death or the chest under the bed. That, for the moment at least, was his secret. When he'd finished, Mr McFadyen shook him by the hand and said, 'Well done, Mr Gold,' and some of his new classmates even applauded.

He lay in bed that night, trying to understand what had happened that morning. Mr McFadyen hadn't even mentioned his stammer, didn't treat him as different, didn't try to help him, didn't ask the others to be especially patient with him. He'd just insisted that he should be treated with the same respect that should be given to everyone. That felt good. It had been a long day and he was tired. Within minutes he was fast asleep.

chapter 10
1963

Despite the wet and blustery weather of a wintry Friday evening in November, Matthew Gold was feeling pleased with life as he walked home past the spot where the house in which he'd been born had once stood. Things had definitely changed for the better in the last few years. Although Pit Road retained its name, it was a very different place from the street in which he'd spent his childhood. The original miners' houses had been demolished at the end of 1960 and replaced eighteen months later by blocks of three-storey flats. There were some elderly folk who lamented the demise of the close-knit mining community, but most people were in no doubt that the comforts of electric lighting and hot water on tap far outweighed the loss of the former way of life with its time-honoured working-class values of industry and neighbourliness. When the demolition had begun, the Golds had been among the first to be rehoused in yet another new council estate half a mile further out of the town, where the flats were built to exactly the same specification as the ones he was now passing.

The changes in Matthew's life, however, went far beyond moving house. He was sixteen years old, no longer a child, increasingly comfortable with his status as a teenager in what the newspapers were beginning to call 'the Swinging Sixties', and considered by his teachers to be one of their most promising students and destined for a place in the English faculty at the University of Glasgow in a couple of years. His growing self-confidence, aided by the speech therapy to which the school had referred him, was manifesting itself in a slight but noticeable decrease in the severity of his stammer. He wasn't free from it by any means, but he'd mastered some useful techniques that helped him cope with it and enabled him to communicate with others without succumbing to panic and embarrassment. With the continuing help of Mr McFadyen, who'd recognised his potential and encouraged him in all things literary, he'd started a book club at the beginning of the term. It had a small but devoted following among those of his peers who were particularly interested in reading, and had given him a certain profile as someone whose opinions – particularly on the merits of detective fiction – were worth hearing. The book club always met after school on Fridays, which was why he was still on his way home at nearly six o'clock.

But there was one particular reason for how he was feeling on this particular evening, significant enough for him to have made a note of it earlier in the day in the journal he'd been keeping for the last year at the suggestion of the man who was not only his English teacher, but who'd become his mentor.

22nd November 1963

At last! I finished reading the last of Grampa's detective novels at dinner time before the first period this afternoon.

Number 51 on the list – DEATH ON THE NILE. Agatha Christie and Hercule Poirot at their best.

It's taken me more than four years to get through them all!

Some of the boys in my class call me Sherlock. (It beats being laughed at for having a stammer.)

I'd no idea Grampa was reading all this stuff when I was a kid.

He must have read them in the morning when he came home from working night shift in the pit, after I went to school and before he went to bed.

Grampa left school at fourteen and I never thought of him reading books.

Mr McFadyen says he's known quite a few miners like that who've worked at educating themselves and who've read a lot.

I wish I'd been able to talk to Grampa about what he was reading. I wonder why he liked detective stories so much. Still miss him.

But it's a day to remember. Not many boys my age have read all this stuff!

Though he couldn't know it at that moment, it would be a day he would remember for other reasons and for the rest of his life, however much he might wish to forget it.

He reached 29C Liberty Court, which he still thought of as 'the new house', just before quarter past six. He climbed the two flights of stairs to the front door, and let himself in.

As usual on a Friday evening, his grandmother was out at one of her Fellowship meetings and his dinner had been left in the oven to keep warm. He spooned a good-sized pile of *stovies* on to a plate, which he quickly cleared before helping himself to a second portion of his favourite meat and potato dish. He finished his meal, made himself a cup of tea and turned on their recently acquired television. His grandmother had initially been reluctant to allow such a 'worldly contraption' into the house, convinced that it was nothing better than an evil device that would insidiously lead to the lowering of moral standards in homes across the nation. It had been the cause of several heated arguments between them until she'd yielded to his contention that it would be beneficial to his education and a help to them both in understanding what was happening in the wider world.

Despite her capitulation on the matter, he wasn't at all sure that she'd been persuaded by his reasoning. Rather, he thought he could detect a slow creeping weariness about her that was gradually eroding her appetite for any kind of confrontation. Their relationship was no warmer than it had ever been but, to his surprise, there had been moments in recent days when he'd found himself almost feeling sorry for her. Her characteristic dogmatic attitude and acerbic tongue seemed to be slowly giving way to a sullen and silent regret. But whatever degree of sympathy he might have felt, his determination to leave home as soon as it was practically possible had never waned.

It was just after seven o'clock when he sat down in front of the television. For all his teenage pretensions to be something of an intellectual and his insistence on the educational advantages of owning a television, what he really liked to watch were sitcoms or, even better, crime shows like *Maigret*. So he was disappointed to discover when he glanced at the *Radio Times* that it was almost time for *Tonight*. It was Friday night, the end of a long school week, and the last thing he needed was a current affairs programme. He was just about to turn it off and go and do something else when, at five minutes past seven, the schedule was interrupted for a newsflash. A solemn-faced man he didn't recognise as one of the regular news readers made the announcement that President John F Kennedy had been shot in Dallas, Texas.

President Kennedy was a hero to Matthew; young, good-looking, passionate about the things that mattered to his generation, and so different from the stuffy old political leaders in his own country. He kept watching when *Tonight* resumed, hoping that there might be more news, better news of the American president. Twenty minutes later the rest of the programme was cancelled and the unfamiliar broadcaster appeared again to inform the audience that President Kennedy had been shot in the head and that his condition was critical. Seconds later the telephone in the studio rang and the news reader paused to answer it. Years later, when he reflected on that moment, Matthew would swear that despite the fact that he was watching on a black-and-white television, he could see the colour drain from the man's face and his expression change as he received and then relayed the news to his viewers: 'We regret to announce that President Kennedy is dead.'

He sat and stared at the screen. The programme schedule was abandoned and for the next nineteen minutes all that viewers across the nation saw was the familiar image that the BBC employed between programmes to identify itself – the icon of a continuously revolving globe. The symbol and the accompanying silence seemed appropriate to Matthew. The world was still spinning on its axis but no one knew what to do or say next. Eventually he stood up, walked slowly across the room and turned off the television. He felt suddenly overwhelmed by the impenetrable mystery of life, by questions to which neither he nor, he suspected, anyone else had any answers. What kind of world was he living in? What was wrong with people that made them want to kill another human being? Why did someone who wanted to make the world better have to die such a violent death?

For the next hour he tried to push such questions out of his mind and distract himself by burying his head in a book. But he'd get to the end of a page and realise that he hadn't taken in one word of what he was reading. He'd just pushed the book aside in frustration for the third time when it occurred to him that his grandmother was usually home by this time. He wondered if they'd heard about the death of President Kennedy at her meeting. Maybe they were praying about it, though he couldn't help thinking that it was a bit late for that. Another half hour went past and she still didn't appear. Now he was beginning to feel worried. She was always up and busy by six in the morning and he could never remember her going to bed later than ten o'clock. Maybe she'd decided to stay overnight with one of her church friends and forgotten to tell him before he left for school. He looked behind the clock on the mantlepiece. That was where she usually left a note to let him know if she was going to be out longer than normal. There was nothing there. He knew in his heart that she would never have considered spending the night anywhere other than at home. That thought, however, brought a glimmer of relief. Why hadn't he thought of it before? Of course – *she must be asleep in her own bed.* She must have been feeling unwell and gone to bed early, as she occasionally did. If she'd taken a couple of her sleeping pills, she'd be dead to the world, sleeping so soundly that she wouldn't have heard him since he got home. He smiled to himself at his stupidity in not realising that earlier.

But just to set his mind at rest, he decided to do something he'd never done before. He'd open the door of her bedroom slightly and look in. Just to check that she was there and everything was fine. He turned the handle as slowly and quietly as he could and peered into the room. The street lamp just outside the window above her bed had gone out the night before and hadn't been fixed yet, so it was difficult to see anything clearly. He narrowed his eyes and stared into the darkness and, to his relief, he could just make out the figure of his grandmother lying on her bed. He was about to close the door and tiptoe away when he had the disturbing sense that everything wasn't quite as it should be. He could sometimes hear her snoring at night, even when his door was closed. But there wasn't a sound coming from the bed. *Something was wrong.* He called out, very softly at first, then louder, 'Granny, are you alright?' There was no reply.

He stood still, uncertain what to do next and vaguely aware that he was beginning to tremble. He forced himself to raise his right hand to turn on the bedroom light. But he hesitated again, afraid of what he might see and unable to control the shaking in his arm. He could never remember how long he stood there before he summoned up the courage to flick the switch. And he could never forget the scene that revealed itself when he eventually managed to carry out that simple action. His grandmother was lying unnaturally still on top of the covers, fully clothed. Her grey hair, which was always swept back severely from her face and tied in a bun behind her head, was lying loose on the pillow. Her face had a deathly pallor, accentuated by the harsh yellow glow from the bulb that hung without a lampshade from the ceiling, and her mouth gaped open as if desperately trying to draw a last despairing breath. And on the bedside cabinet to her left was an empty bottle of aspirin and an almost empty bottle of whisky.

For a moment his mind was unable to comprehend what must have happened. Then the horror of what he was looking at smashed into him with the force of a gigantic wave, knocking him to his hands and knees and leaving him feeling completely disorientated. The ugly reality of untimely death with which he was now confronted was hideously different from the sanitised descriptions of such events in the murder mysteries he'd been devouring so avidly. He pulled himself to his feet and rushed to the bathroom, where he dropped to his knees again and was violently sick into the lavatory. Without fully realising what he was doing, he stood up, washed his face, rinsed his mouth, and walked across the landing to the adjoining flat. He knocked on the door and waited for what seemed an age for someone to answer. When his neighbour, who had been asleep, eventually appeared in her dressing gown, he looked at her and said very slowly and deliberately but, to his surprise, without even a hint of a stammer, 'I think my granny is dead. Please can you call the police?' Then he fainted.

chapter 11
1963–1964

It was two o'clock on Friday 20th December, the last school day at Bellmill Academy before the term ended and the Christmas holidays began. An unmistakably festive atmosphere had already made meaningful work impossible. Mrs Smith, the normally busy school secretary, was salving her conscience by making sure the office would be left tidy while she sang along with The Beatles' latest number one hit that was playing on the transistor radio on the corner of her desk. She smiled wistfully to herself as she sang that she wanted to hold someone's hand. Having lived alone for the last twenty years since her boys had left home and her husband had died, hand-holding was not an activity she had indulged in for a very long time.

She realised with a start that someone was banging on the office door. Whoever it was must have been knocking for some time, but she'd been so caught up in her singing and tidying that she'd been oblivious to the divergent rhythm being beaten on her door until it became too loud and insistent to ignore. She turned off the radio, quickly assumed her customary diligent and professional bearing, and called out in as formal a voice as she could manage, 'Come in, please.' The door opened slowly and a dishevelled-looking boy in his mid-teens entered the room and stared at her with an expression on his face that suggested he was only just managing to stay awake. For a moment or two she wondered who on earth the person standing in front of her could be. But as soon as he began to speak, she recognised her unexpected visitor immediately.

'P-p-please, Mmmmrs Ssssmith, I'd lllike to sssee Mmmr M-M-McFadyen.'

'Oh, Matthew Gold, thank God you're safe,' she replied, sitting him down on a chair. 'We've all been so worried about you. Stay there and I'll fetch Mr McFadyen for you right away.'

Mrs Smith was the kind of school secretary whose influence had increased steadily over the years that she'd worked at Bellmill Academy until her authority far surpassed her official status in the staff hierarchy. She was used to her commands being obeyed, and her precisely delivered instruction to an unsuspecting pupil who was passing along the corridor outside her office to 'fetch Mr McFadyen without delay' produced immediate results. Within minutes the head of the English Department was sitting alongside her while they both listened intently as Matthew explained, as best he could, his whereabouts for the past month and what had happened to him since the night he'd discovered his grandmother's body.

After he'd recovered consciousness from fainting and been briefly interviewed by the two police officers who'd responded quickly to the summons, he'd spent the night asleep on the couch in his neighbours' home. Early the next morning, well before they were awake, he'd got out of bed and gone back into his grandmother's house. He couldn't remember exactly why he'd done that, other than that he was probably thinking that he ought to change his clothes and collect some things. But as soon as he entered the house, he realised to his dismay that his grandmother's body was still lying in her bedroom. He was struck by an irresistible panic. His mind was racing and the only thought that would come into clear focus was that he had to get out of there, get as far away as he could as quickly as possible. But he'd only two shillings and some pennies in his pocket. Where could he get some money? He forced himself to breathe more slowly and told himself to calm down and think. That's what Grampa had always told him to do…

Thinking about Grampa was enough to remind him that he knew where he could find some money. When they'd moved from Pit Road to Liberty Court, he'd insisted, despite his grandmother's protests, on bringing Grampa's chest and putting it at the foot of his bed. His grandmother never wanted to look at it, never mind touch it, so he knew it was a safe place in which to hide anything he wanted to keep secret and secure. He slipped his hand into a space between his bed and the wall and retrieved the old brass key that he kept concealed there. He unlocked the chest and fumbled between the books that he still kept there until he felt what he was looking for – Grampa's tobacco tin. His fingers felt clumsy as he prised it open and took out something that had remained in the tin untouched since the day he'd found it. It was something that belonged to Grampa, something that he had no right to use. But today he was sure Grampa would understand. It was still dark when he slipped quietly out of the house with only the clothes he was wearing – a T-shirt, a blue anorak, his old grey school trousers – and a pair of black canvas plimsolls on his feet. And in his pocket was Grampa's £5 note.

He had very little memory of the first few days apart from getting on and off buses, sleeping out in the open and being constantly cold. Somehow or other he'd linked up with a group of teenagers he'd met in Glasgow, most of whom were two or three years older than he was, who were squatting in an unoccupied tenement that was due for demolition. Having learned that he was willing to contribute the £4 he still had to their communal pot of money, they welcomed him into their unstructured and easy-going community without question. With his only previous sortie into the world of teenage rebellion having been a quick cigarette behind the school toilets, their uninhibited attitude towards casual sex and their use of illegal drugs had shocked and disturbed him. But the refuge it offered from an even more confusing adult world outside, and the respite their company afforded him from having to deal with the consequences of his grandmother's suicide, made it easier to stay where he was than to venture back into the harsh reality from which he'd fled.

How long he might have remained there, he'd no idea. But, by the end of the third week, he began to notice that as his money was decreasing, so was their laid-back acceptance of his presence. Things came to a head when one of the group returned one day waving the front page of an old tabloid newspaper he'd found while rummaging through some stuff in a house that had recently become vacant and which he was checking out as a possible upgrade on their present squat. It was dated Monday 25th November 1963 and carried a photograph of a boy in school uniform under the headline 'SCHOOLBOY MISSING AFTER DISCOVERING GRANDMOTHER'S BODY'. The boy in the photograph was identified in the article as 'sixteen-year-old Matthew Gold'. The attitude of the others towards him changed immediately. And when a heated argument broke out as to whether his presence increased the risk of the premises being raided by the police, Matthew took the opportunity to slip away as quietly as he could before things turned nasty.

He spent that night on a park bench, huddled in an old sleeping bag he'd managed to take from the squat, but it was no match for the bitter chill of winter. He slept only fitfully and woke up feeling cold, stiff and hungry. He knew that whatever awaited him, he had to go back. With no money left in Grampa's tin in his pocket, he walked the twelve miles from Glasgow to Bellmill. Going home was not an option. The only place he could go, if he could get there before it was locked up for the holidays, was school. He hoped that somebody there would understand and help him.

He reached the end of his story and tears began to flow down his face. The effort of the day and the events of the past month had left him physically and emotionally exhausted. He was surprised when Mrs Smith, who had a hard-earned and well-deserved reputation for having no patience with anyone who came to her office with elaborate excuses or long tales of woe, reached out and held his hand.

'You've been through a lot, Matthew,' she said in a voice that was very different from her normal brusque speech. 'Just sit there quietly for a moment while Mr McFadyen and I have a chat about what we need to do.'

Before she and Mr McFadyen stepped outside the door and into the corridor, she opened her handbag and passed him a soft cotton handkerchief to dry his tears. He hadn't touched anything as clean and smooth as that for a very long time. Just holding it in his hands was enough to release a flood of emotion that he'd kept dammed up for the past month. He was glad to be left on his own long enough so that no one could see him sobbing in a way he hadn't done since he was a little child. The door opened again and the two adults came back into the room. He wiped his eyes with Mrs Smith's handkerchief and looked at them, wondering what they'd been talking about and what they were about to say. Mrs Smith sat opposite him and Mr McFadyen perched on her desk and dangled his legs, just as he'd see him do on his first day at school. It was a sight he found comforting. It made him feel that someone he could trust was taking control of the situation.

'Matthew, we've chatted to each other and we've managed to get hold of the headmaster for a couple of minutes. Here's what we've agreed between us. We'll contact the police to let them know that you're back. And the doctor will want to take a look at you and make sure you're alright after all you've been through. But we need to talk about where you can stay until things can be sorted out.'

It suddenly occurred to him that he hadn't given any thought to such practicalities. It had taken all the mental effort he could summon just to get himself back to Bellmill. Mr McFadyen gave him a reassuring smile.

'How would you feel about this? Mrs Smith has a spare room and an extra bathroom and she's very willing to have you stay for the next few weeks. That would give us the opportunity to work out what's best for you.'

He thought he was going to start crying all over again and he was grateful when Mr McFadyen resumed what he was saying.

'It's only a couple of days to Christmas, of course. She's a great cook and she'll get you fattened up again before New Year.'

'And, Matthew,' Mrs Smith interjected with a chuckle, 'you don't need to worry. I'm not always the dictator you see here at school. I've brought up two boys like you, though it was a long time ago. You'll be alright. I promise you.'

'Th-th-thank you,' he stammered, unsure of how to react or what else to say.

That afternoon, after everyone else except the janitor had left the building and the secretary's office was tidied and locked up for the holidays, Matthew Gold went home with Mrs Martha Smith, the hard-working widowed mother of two grown-up sons. When those sons and their wives and children came to spend Christmas Day with their mother, they didn't seem to find his presence at all unusual and welcomed him as part of the family. When he tried to tell them how grateful he was for her kindness they just smiled and said, 'She's been bringing people home since we were kids. She likes people to think she's a tough old boot, but she's really a bit of a softy.'

What was originally intended to be a brief stay stretched into weeks. Martha Smith kept a close eye on his physical and emotional welfare and supported him as he dealt with the ongoing consequences of his grandmother's death. She helped him through the funeral, which had been delayed because of his disappearance, and she arranged for one of her sons to clear his grandmother's council house and dispose of everything except the chest of books, which she made sure was put safely in his room. For a time, they talked in general terms about where he might find accommodation, but it became clear that the existing arrangement suited them both. A bond of mutual respect and affection that neither of them wanted to break had been forged between them. The weeks turned into months, and before the end of March, with the ready approval of the authorities, a widow nearing retirement had become the legal guardian of a teenage boy she'd grown to love as much as her own sons.

The official confirmation of their new relationship arrived in the post as they were finishing breakfast on a Saturday morning, with The Beatles' latest release, 'Can't Buy Me Love', playing on the radio. Matthew wondered aloud why the woman he'd quickly come to call 'Ma' was adding her lilting Scottish brogue to the Scouse accents of the four Liverpudlians. He hadn't thought of pop music being her thing. She smiled at him and told him that despite her age, she rather liked The Beatles. She also told him the title of the song she'd been singing along with on the afternoon just before Christmas when he'd turned up unexpectedly at her office: 'I Want to Hold Your Hand'.

'You know,' she added thoughtfully, 'they're singing just the right song again. I'd been thinking that maybe it was time to retire, spend some of what I've got saved on a long holiday, or buy myself something nice. But actually, this is better than anything I could have bought.'

chapter 12
1965

Matthew Gold caught sight of his reflection in one of the shop windows as he walked up Sauchiehall Street on a late October morning in 1965. He liked what he saw. His haversack casually slung over his right shoulder, his Arts Faculty scarf with its distinctive purple and yellow colours draped round his neck, and his green corduroy jacket recently purchased with his student grant, would be enough to ensure that everyone who saw him would know that this was a young man on his way to the University of Glasgow. He was eighteen, it was his second month of student life and, at last, he felt he'd begun to break free and be his true self. Mr McFadyen had tutored him closely in his final year at Bellmill Academy and his exam results had been more than good enough to secure him a place to study English Language and Literature. And Ma Smith's provision of a good home had given him a solid base from which he could set out on adult life. Schooldays and childhood were behind him.

Of course, like many of his fellow students in the surrounding towns, he was still living at home and travelling into Glasgow every day. But that only added to his sense of liberation from the confines of the coal-mining town in which he had grown up and from which he made his escape four or five times a week. Each morning he'd walk to Bellmill Station, catch the 8.15 train to Glasgow Central and – if it wasn't raining – rather than catch a bus, he'd walk the two miles up Sauchiehall Street, along Woodlands Road and through Kelvingrove Park. And when he reached University Avenue and passed through the wrought-iron gates, he always felt as if he was entering another world. He knew that, in reality, the building dated only from the end of the nineteenth century and was less than 100 years old. But the dark and dramatic Gothic Revivalist style of its architecture created a sense of ages long past. He imagined that if the stones could talk, they would impart deep wisdom and reveal hidden mysteries of which he as yet knew little.

On this particular morning there was a touch of warmth in the winter sunshine and he'd allowed himself to dally a little. As a consequence, his walk had taken him several minutes longer than usual. He hurried through the Cloisters and across the West Quadrangle to the large lecture hall where Simon Ramsey, a junior lecturer reputed to be something of a rising star in academic circles, was delivering the third in his series of lectures on the Romantic poets. That his lectures were always well attended owed at least as much to the fact that the female half of the student body, to whom he was known as 'Si the guy', considered him to be exceptionally good-looking.

By the time Matthew got there, the lecture had already begun and the front rows were filled, leaving him with no option but to climb the steps all the way to the back of the lecture theatre. His efforts to tread lightly on the wooden floorboards and make as little noise as possible were thwarted when he tripped over a bag lying on the steps. His fall would have been sufficiently noisy in itself to disrupt the lecture. But the raucous cheering and stamping of his fellow students at his mishap brought the procedure to a halt, much to the annoyance of the lecturer who'd been enjoying the hitherto rapt attention of his audience. Trying to cover his embarrassment and ignore the hilarity his fall had provoked, Matthew picked himself up, found a seat at the end of the row and pulled his pad out of his haversack ready to take notes. The ironic applause subsided, eventually to be replaced by a tense silence that made his embarrassment all the more acute. When Simon Ramsey began to speak again it was obvious that he had not appreciated the interruption to his presentation. His previously authoritative tone had assumed a more sarcastic edge and it seemed to Matthew that he'd not only failed to see the humour in the situation, but that he'd spotted an opportunity to impress his female admirers.

'I would be grateful if students would ensure that they arrive in good time for my lectures.' He raised his eyes from the handwritten manuscript on the desk in front of him and looked up to the back row. 'And I would also appreciate it if the gentleman whose late arrival has caused such disturbance would wait behind and speak to me at the end of this lecture.'

For the next forty-five minutes Matthew tried to concentrate and take notes on what was being said from the podium concerning the reaction of the Romantic poets to the cold rationalism of their neo-classical predecessors. It was all to no avail. He was becoming more anxious and distracted with every minute that passed. By the time everyone else had left and he was making his way down to the front of the lecture hall, the confident swagger with which he had strolled up Sauchiehall Street had completely deserted him. He mounted the steps to the platform and stood awkwardly, unsure of the etiquette he should be observing at such a moment. Simon Ramsey remained seated on the raised stool beside the lectern.

'And what might your name be?'

The question was delivered in the weary manner of an adult dealing with an annoying child and it knocked that last ounce of confidence out of Matthew. He felt like he was six years old, back in Bellmill Primary. He tried to control his breathing before he spoke.

'M-M-Mmmatthew G-G-Gold.'

Mr Ramsey ran his finger down a typed sheet of paper on the table. When he glanced up there was the merest hint of a smirk on his face.

'Ah yes. Mmmatthew Gold. I've got it...'

There was a little part of Matthew that couldn't help admiring the cunning of the man – the way he kept his lips together on the letter M, stretching out the sound as if he was searching the list for his name. But his grudging admiration served only to make his anger all the more intense. Simon Ramsey was mocking him. Something inside him snapped at that moment. In the sneering features of the man sitting in front of him he could see the faces of Miss Prinn and Danny Johnstone and everyone else who'd ridiculed him and mimicked his stammer. A rage that had been suppressed for years broke to the surface. He was powerless to resist it as it swept away the barriers of restraint and embarrassment that had held it back for so long. Without being fully in control of what he was doing and without allowing his stammer to inhibit him, he aimed a torrent of expletive-filled abuse at the man sitting in front of him. Who did he think he was? He knew perfectly well that what had happened was just an accident. He was using it as a chance to show off and impress the girls in the room. Mocking someone's stammer only showed how immature and contemptible he was. He was a disgrace to the university…

On and on it went, and by the time he eventually came to a halt, Matthew could see that Simon Ramsey was no longer *Si the guy*. He was a frightened man who was taken aback by the reaction his casual contempt had provoked. His face was pale and his hands were shaking. He got down from his stool unsteadily and tried to gather up his notes into his briefcase. He made a last effort to regain control of the situation.

'You'll hear more about this outburst,' he said, trying to assume the nonchalant manner with which he'd delivered his lecture. 'I'm going to make a full report on your behaviour in the lecture and on your unprovoked verbal attack on me.'

'D-d-do whatever y-y-ou like. Yyyou dis-g-gust me.'

Matthew turned around and hurried out of the room, pausing only as he reached the door to suggest to the flustered academic an alternative place where he might think of putting his report rather than presenting it to the university authorities. As he walked back across the quadrangle and through the Cloisters, his anger began to subside, only to be replaced by a gnawing concern regarding the consequences of the confrontation that had just happened. The possibility that he might be thrown out of university was too terrible to contemplate. That would mean letting down all the people who'd helped him and had faith in him – people like Grampa and Mrs Evans and Mr McFadyen and Ma Smith. But even that disturbing thought could not break his resolve that he would neither back down nor apologise to someone who had treated him as contemptuously as Simon Ramsey had just done. Not now. And not any time in the future.

chapter 13
1966

It was just before nine o'clock on a warm sunny morning at the end of May when Matthew Gold took his place with 100 or so fellow students for the final exam of his first year at university. Even a dramatic improvement in the weather in the last two days had done nothing to lighten his mood. Just the thought of spending two hours trying to write something meaningful about Elizabethan dramatists was enough to dampen his spirits. Analysing stuff that had been written four centuries ago wasn't something for which he could summon up any enthusiasm. And whose bright idea had it been that the Bute Hall was a conducive place in which to think and work? He hated the Bute Hall. Early in his first semester he'd been taken on a conducted tour of the campus by an overenthusiastic guide who'd described it as 'the architectural jewel in the crown of Glasgow university'. To him it was more like those cheap and gaudy glass trinkets people bought on a seaside holiday. The initial impact that the Gothic Revivalist architecture had made on him in his first weeks as an undergraduate had gradually given way to a growing irritation at what he'd come to think of as a tasteless pastiche.

He took his pen out of his pocket, set it down on the desk, and looked around. The pointed arches and tall cast-iron columns decorated with what looked like fake heraldic motifs in lurid colours now seemed ridiculous to him. And the heavy, pendulous light fittings – which the guide had said were designed to resemble the head of the University Mace – left him lost for words. Even the stained-glass windows commemorating a procession of academics, saints and monarchs seemed out of sync with life in the middle of the twentieth century. It was 1966, the Swinging Sixties, the sun was shining outside, and he was imprisoned in a room that was stuck in the past.

His earlier dream that if the stones could talk, they would teach him something of the mystery and meaning of life had vanished. In truth, they were nothing more than a bogus façade. The only thing they had to say was, 'None of this is real. It's all a pretence.' And what was the point of it all? What was the point in pretending you're still living in the Middle Ages? Come to think of it, what was the point of university? Of anything?

The boredom he was feeling, the sense that there wasn't any real purpose to what he was doing had been growing ever since his clash with Simon Ramsey. His fears about whatever action might be taken against him had quickly disappeared. An informal and brief interview with a senior member of the faculty had left him in little doubt that *Si the guy*'s peers found him as unpleasant as he did and that this wasn't the first time his arrogant manner had provoked a confrontation with a student. He was let off with a mild rebuke relating to the use of profanities on the campus and told that since this was a one-off occurrence, there would be no further disciplinary action. But the incident had changed his view of the value of academic success. If someone could pass all the exams and work his way through the system to teach in a university and still be a conceited fool like Simon Ramsey, it wasn't worth the effort.

His shifting outlook had an inevitable impact on his work. He still travelled into Glasgow every day, still attended lectures and tutorials, still handed in his essays. But his heart wasn't in it. He read and studied little and his lack of interest was soon reflected in his grades. Ma Smith had picked up on his change of attitude and asked Mr McFadyen to speak to him. They'd had a long conversation and he'd promised to get back into his studies and turn things around. He'd really meant what he said and for a time, things were better. But he had neither the energy nor the resolve to keep it up. Within a few weeks he'd slipped back to merely going through the motions without actually doing any real work.

The notes he took in lectures bore no relation to what was being delivered from the front of the room. Instead, he filled the time by writing about his fellow students. As the months passed, he'd withdrawn more and more into himself, and his increasing isolation meant that he didn't know any of them well. But that suited his purposes. The people sitting around him merged into the fog of confusion and contradiction that university life had become, and slowly but surely he retreated from the world of reality and reason into a parallel realm of fantasy and imagination. He focused his attention on anyone who particularly drew his interest. The Jesuit priest and the arrestingly beautiful Irish girl with whom he came to lectures every day became the Priest and the Princess; the mature student in his mid-forties whose hair was greying at the temples was christened Old Dan Grey; the ex-professional footballer preparing for a second career in teaching took on the role of a hard-drinking compulsive gambler struggling to break free from his addictions; the fresh-faced young woman with the soft Highland accent was identified in his imagination as a twentieth-century reincarnation of Mary Morrison, the Ayrshire beauty who won the heart of Robert Burns.

Normally, he carried an A4 pad with pages crammed with such fictions. But this was an exam. A day of reckoning. And, as the clock on the university tower struck the quarter hour at 9.15, all that lay on his desk was an exam paper with five questions and several sheets of lined paper on which to write his answers. He turned over the paper and read the first question:

> *With reference to Shakespeare's Henry IV and Marlowe's Tamburlaine, discuss the following statement: Elizabethan drama is a creative combination of history, polemic and fiction.*

His irritation morphed into anger. He didn't have a clue what the answer was to that question. And what difference would it make if he did? He wanted to stand up and tell everybody in the hall that Shakespeare and Marlowe wouldn't have cared either. They were writing plays that would vie with bear-baiting and other popular pastimes for the attention of ordinary people. Plays that were full of life and energy. Now we're sat here dissecting them like some kind of dead animal in a laboratory, he thought. And the only way you can do that is by killing the poor creatures. Just like we're killing these plays.

He glanced at the figures on either side of him, bent over their desks and already beginning to write furiously. He leaned back in his chair and gazed up at the stained-glass windows and ornate balcony that surrounded three sides of the hall. He leaned a little further back in his chair and looked at the lights dangling from the ceiling and started to laugh quietly to himself. After a few minutes, he sat up straight, put his pen back in his pocket, stood up, and cleared his throat.

'That's it,' he said in a voice loud enough to be sure he could be heard in every corner of the hall. 'I can't take any more of this. It's a waste of time.'

He picked up the exam paper and slowly ripped it into tiny pieces, letting them fall over his desk. The invigilator called out, telling him to sit down and be quiet. But there was no chance of that happening. He was still shouting as he strode to the door.

'My name's Matthew Gold and you'll find my answers on the desk.'

It was only when the door slammed closed behind him and he began to run down the stairs and out through the quadrangle that two things dawned on him. It was the first thing he'd said in his time at university without stammering. And it was the second time in his life that he'd run away. But this time he knew there would be no going home.

mystery man

1966-1996

portraits of an aspiring writer

chapter 14
1966

Even making beans on toast was a slow and frustrating job when the tin-opener didn't grip properly, the grill above the cooker was faulty, and only one of the gas rings on the stove top was still working. But at least his two flatmates with whom he shared the tiny kitchen had gone out for the evening, leaving him the place to himself. Besides which, it was the end of the week and he didn't have enough money left to make his usual trip to the fish and chip shop on the other side of the street for his main meal of the day. He took his make-do dinner and a mug of tea and put them down carefully on the unsteady Formica-topped table in his room. The end of his bed had to do service as a substitute for the single folding chair that had collapsed under his weight a few days earlier. He ate in silence and reflected on his situation.

The question was: what to do now? The adrenalin rush of his dramatic exit from the Bute Hall had long since passed. There had been, Matthew could see with the benefit of hindsight, more than a touch of bravado in the role of the Angry Young Man he'd played with such panache when walking out of the exam room with a shout of protest against what he saw as the pretentiousness of academic life. There was, however, nothing heroic or glamorous about living in a damp and dingy flat above a launderette in one of the poorest areas of Glasgow with no income other than social security payments and the occasional casual work where employers were willing to pay cash in hand. Six months of this kind of life was long enough and he promised himself that in the morning he'd shake off the lethargy that still hung over him and look for a proper job.

A week after he walked out of the Bute Hall, he'd written to Ma Smith and Mr McFadyen letting them know what had happened and telling them that he wouldn't be coming home. He apologised for the disappointment he knew his decision to drop out of university would cause them; he tried to explain that he needed time and space to sort himself out; and he asked them not to come looking for him or contact him. His mind was a hotchpotch of confused thoughts and conflicting ideas: what was he going to do with his life? Was he forever going to be defined and confined by his stammer? How could he make any sense of life when it seemed to be a random assortment of meaningless tragedies? His teenage mother had died while giving him birth, his grampa had suffered a fatal heart attack when Matthew was still a child, and his grandmother had taken her own life. Why did it all happen to him? Was there something about him that brought bad luck or some kind of curse on anyone who got close to him? And what harm might he bring to decent people like Ma

Smith and Mr McFadyen, who'd shown such kindness to him, if he stayed around?

Before they'd gone out earlier in the evening, Tom, one of his flatmates, remarked half-jokingly that if he was really as fed up as he looked, he needed to either 'see a shrink or get religion'. The unsuspecting young man was taken aback by the vehemence of the anger his comment provoked. Matthew told him in no uncertain terms that he wasn't mad and he definitely wasn't about to see a psychiatrist. And forget religion! He'd been brought up by a crazy, church-going grandmother, and he'd had enough religion to last a lifetime. And, as for comments like that, he should keep them to himself in future.

'Then you'd better start sorting yourself out, mate,' Tom replied. ''Cos you're becoming hard work to live with. You'll make us as miserable as yourself if we're not careful.'

And that casual remark had just set the whole crazy carousel of questions spinning round in his head all over again.

He took his plate and mug and put them in the sink on the top of the stack of dirty dishes that were waiting for whoever had the time or inclination to do the washing-up. He thought about doing it himself, changed his mind, and then changed it again. Why not do something nice for his mates, if they were finding him such hard work to live with? At least it would help pass the time on a dreary November night. It took a good forty minutes to wash and dry and put away a week's worth of greasy plates and saucepans. He even wiped around the edges of the sink and added the now sopping wet tea towel to the pile that needed to be taken down to the launderette in the morning. Whether it was the meal he'd just eaten or the fact that the flat looked a shade tidier than it had done, he felt his spirits lift a little.

It was still only nine o'clock, too early to think about going to bed. The black-and-white television they'd bought for a few pounds from a second-hand electrical shop had only a wire coat hanger for an aerial which meant that at best the reception was fuzzy and at worst it would lose the signal completely, usually at a crucial moment in the programme. So, having taken himself to task and made his resolution to look for work in the morning, he decided that rather than fight a losing battle with the TV, he'd do something he hadn't done since he'd left university. He'd read a book. The problem was all of his books were still at Ma Smith's and there wasn't anything he considered decent reading material in the flat.

Then he remembered that he'd once picked up a paperback edition of an American detective story that Tom had been reading. It had led to a heated argument between them on the merits or otherwise of the American hard-boiled crime fiction that appealed to Tom but that Matthew dismissed as cheap and nasty after a brief and cursory glance at the first few pages. The mean and violent streets of Chicago and Los Angeles were far less appealing to him than the grand country houses and leafy lanes of rural England where Lord Peter Wimsey or Father Brown practised and honed their powers of deduction. And the cynical, smart-talking gumshoes who plied their trade in those streets were even less like their more cerebral and sophisticated European counterparts, idealistic amateurs who would never have dreamed of accepting payment for their efforts to see wrongdoers punished and those who had been wrongly accused set free.

But, since there was nothing else around, maybe he'd take another look, just to fill in the time and occupy his mind for an hour or so. He wandered into Tom's room and found what he was looking for. There must have been twenty-five or thirty dog-eared paperbacks lying in an untidy heap in the corner of the room. He glanced at the titles one after another, throwing each one back on the floor until he came to one that looked substantial enough to offer a couple of hours reading – *The Big Sleep* by Raymond Chandler. He vaguely knew the author's name, though he'd never read any of his books. At least, he thought to himself, it's an appropriate title. If nothing else it'll put me to sleep and offer the possibility of a restful night.

He hadn't got beyond the first few pages when he grudgingly acknowledged that 'the man knows how to write'. After half an hour, he couldn't put it down. His flatmates came home just after midnight and he was still reading. And at half past three in the morning, long after they'd gone to bed, he finished the final chapter. He closed the book and lay back on his bed, gazing up at the ceiling. Why hadn't he read this stuff before? Why had he been so arrogant as to dismiss something he'd never read as lowbrow pulp fiction unworthy of his attention? He'd thought he knew a thing or two about detective fiction. But this was unlike all the books in Grampa's chest. And Philip Marlowe was different from the somewhat eccentric and genteel figures who inhabited their pages and investigated crimes with a cool detachment. For a start, Marlowe was a red-blooded male. Dressed in his black brogues and powder-blue suit with its stylish pocket handkerchief, he was both attractive and attracted to the opposite sex. And, unlike his well-to-do counterparts in England who could afford to wait for calls from wealthy clients or had enough leisure time to join the affluent guests at house parties in country estates, Marlowe was neither embarrassed to admit he needed money nor reluctant to go looking for work wherever he could find it.

But what really captured Matthew's attention was that, whereas the exploits of Sherlock Holmes and Father Brown and Hercule Poirot were all related in the third person, Raymond Chandler made *his* detective the narrator. The story was told and the action was observed and described by Marlowe himself. And his words were an intoxicating verbal cocktail of world-weary cynicism and wise-cracking commentary, shaken together with a generous dash of slang-peppered dialogue. No painter could have depicted the scenes more vividly or drawn the characters in sharper relief than Marlowe did. His extravagant and wildly imaginative similes were like shafts of sunlight, illuminating and highlighting details that would otherwise have seemed insignificant and been overlooked.

It was five o'clock in the morning before he eventually began to drift off to sleep. Since the day he found Grampa's chest under the bed, he'd loved crime fiction. But he'd never imagined that it was a genre that could arouse such conflicting emotions of admiration for the technique of the writer and envy of the character he'd created. It was ridiculous, he knew, but he had to admit it: he was envious of a fictional character. Try as he might, he couldn't shake off the feeling. *He wanted to be like Philip Marlowe!* Marlowe was everything that he wasn't – a good looker, a sharp dresser, a smart talker. A man of the world who could summon up the answers to the questions that a confused and corrupt world threw at him. And here *he* was, lying on his bed in a depressing room feeling a complete failure. A man whose stupid, embarrassing stammer too often shut him off from the rest of the world. A loner who seemed to bring bad luck to anyone who got near him and tried to help him. A drop-out from university with no job, no prospects and no answers to the questions that wouldn't go away.

For all that, he was glad he'd picked the book up and read it. Even deeper than either his admiration for the author or his envy of his hero was the sense that, not for the first time in his life, he'd glimpsed the truth that the world was not without mystery, but neither was it without meaning. It stirred within him memories of days long ago. He could see the little boy sitting with his grampa in Mr Verricchia's Ice Cream Parlour listening to the music coming from the gramophone in the corner that seemed to call him to places far distant and infinitely desirable. And he could hear again the mysterious words he'd sung in school assembly – 'By cool Siloam's shady rill…' They were nothing like the words in the book he'd just read. But they carried the same warning note and the same tantalising summons. It was a warning and a summons that a boy with a stammer could perhaps hear more clearly than anyone else. *Finding the right words and addressing them to others will always be one of our greatest challenges. But learn to use them well and they will draw us together and take us to places we could never otherwise reach.*

chapter 15
1981

Fifteen years was a long time. The town had changed little since that May morning in 1966 when he'd boarded the train for Glasgow expecting to be back in Ma Smith's house the same evening. But he hadn't gone back. Not on that or any other evening. Going back and facing the people he'd let down was something he just couldn't make himself do. And as time passed, the thought of returning became ever more difficult. After the first few years, he got in touch from time to time, writing the occasional letter and letting them know where he was and how things were going. He'd even started to send presents every Christmas to Mr McFadyen and Ma Smith. It made him feel a little less guilty for his sudden disappearance and he hoped it would at least show them that he was grateful for what they'd done for him. But he couldn't bring himself to go back. Not until he'd got the message telling him that Ma was dying of cancer. He knew he had to go and see her. Even then, he delayed and delayed to the point where he'd left it too late to see her alive and had to settle for arriving just in time for her funeral.

Bellmill Cemetery looked and felt just the same as when he'd been there for the funerals of his grandparents. Set as it was on the edge of the town with nothing to shelter it from the cold wind that often blew in from the north, even on warmer days it was a place that could cause you to shiver. Today, as he stood with the other mourners around the open grave on a typical March afternoon, the wind and driving horizontal rain were making it almost impossible to stand upright. Despite his long absence and what some of those standing near him saw as his selfishness and ingratitude to the woman who'd taken him into her home, he'd been accorded the honour, at Ma's express wish, along with her two sons, Mr McFadyen his old English teacher, and four other close friends, of holding one of the cords that would lower her coffin into the grave.

The undertaker pulled away the slats that were holding the casket in place and they began to lower it slowly. His tears mingled with the rain that was running down his face, and that was the first time in those fifteen long years since he'd walked out of the Bute Hall that Matthew had cried for what he had lost and left behind: a secure home where he'd been welcomed; a good woman who'd loved him as she loved her own sons; a family in which he would have been regarded as a brother; a town in which he would have had an identity and in which he might have played a significant role. And what had he traded those things for? A moment of youthful bravado and more than a decade of trying to find who he was and where he belonged. Emotionally he was stateless, a displaced person condemned to a futile search for a purpose that would give his life some meaning.

They gathered in Ma Smith's house for some refreshments after the committal. Standing close to the fireplace to dry out his rain-soaked clothes and holding his hands tightly round his cup of tea to get some warmth back into them, he tried to find the right words to apologise to one of her sons for his failure to visit. He shook his head and put his hand on Matthew's arm.

'You don't need to apologise or explain,' he said with a smile that reminded Matthew of Ma. 'Of course, she was disappointed that you didn't come home. She missed you terribly and worried about you a lot. But she wouldn't let anybody say a word against you. She'd just tell anybody who dared to criticise you that she knew you meant no disrespect and that none of them had come through what you'd had to deal with in your life.'

Mr McFadyen, who'd been standing with them, pulled a neat brown paper parcel out of a bag he was holding and handed it to Matthew.

'Before she died, she gave this to me and told me to be sure to pass it on to you if ever I saw you. It was very special to her and she wanted you to have it. But you might want to wait until you're on your own before you open it.'

Matthew mumbled his thanks and the conversation moved on to more general topics and memories of his time at Bellmill Academy and as an adopted member of the Smith family. He took time to speak briefly to one or two other people who remembered him before excusing himself and heading back to the station to catch a train.

As the train from Bellmill passed through the stations whose names had once been so familiar to him on his daily journey into Glasgow Central station, he couldn't help but reflect on how his life had changed since those days. The resolution he'd made in that ghastly flat above the launderette on the November night back in 1966 to find himself a regular job had proved to be more than mere good intentions. He'd found employment the next day and had hardly been out of work since, though all of the jobs he'd done were menial, low-paid employment, either manual labour or in a variety of industries where no specific skills were required and where the extra payment for working night shift made up for the unsociable hours. None of them presented him with anything that remotely resembled career prospects, but that hadn't worried him at all. They'd provided him with sufficient income to cover the cost of a decent bedsit where he could live on his own. And, more importantly, they'd left him with enough mental and emotional energy to spend his time writing.

Work definitely wasn't the important thing in his life; never more than a means to provide enough money to allow him to follow his passion. The impact of his first encounter with Philip Marlowe on that same November night had rekindled the youthful ambition that the detached and critical approach demanded from someone studying English at university had all but quenched in him. *He wanted to be a writer.* More particularly, he wanted to be a writer of detective fiction, to create a character who would embody the spirit of the time and who would expose the corrupt underbelly of life in Britain in the second half of the twentieth century just as Chandler's hero had done for America in the 1930s. He'd given himself enthusiastically to the task, painstakingly writing and rewriting three separate novels, each with a different central character in the role of crime-solver. He'd sent them to twenty different publishers, only to have them all rejected. Usually it was the standard rejection letter with the same bland wording, which made him wonder if they'd even bothered to look at his manuscript. But occasionally he'd receive a letter making specific reference to what he'd actually written. His writing showed signs of real promise, they said, but his plots were run-of-the-mill and his detective lacked a distinctive persona that would capture the readers' attention. One publisher told him bluntly: 'We receive hundreds of manuscripts just like this every year. You need to come up with a fresh twist for us to be interested.'

In his heart he knew that they were right. His efforts were workmanlike, but utterly lacking in the spark that would bring the story to life and enable the cast of characters to step off the page. And he tried everything he could think of to break through whatever was holding him back. He invested some of his hard-earned money in enrolling in creative writing courses, where he picked up useful tips, but never that missing ingredient that would make his books, if not bestsellers, at least interesting enough to grab the attention of a publisher. It became an obsession to the point where he embarked on what was almost an itinerant lifestyle. He left Glasgow after a couple of years and lived for six or nine months in a succession of cities – Edinburgh, Belfast, Aberdeen, Birmingham, London, Portsmouth, Norwich, Leeds, Liverpool, Southampton – trying to absorb the local culture in the hope it would provide the inspiration he was looking for. He became skilled at quickly finding work and cheap accommodation, but not, alas, in discovering the missing element from his writing. He'd eventually ended up in Manchester, where he'd been living for the past two years. And it was for the name of that city that he scoured the destination boards when he arrived at Glasgow Central station.

His train wouldn't leave for another hour and a half, so he bought himself a newspaper, ordered a pot of tea and a sandwich, and found himself a table in the station café. Most of what was in the newspaper was just the passing trivia of the day, the kind of thing he could read in a couple of minutes and still be none the wiser about anything by the time he got to the end of it. There were two articles, however, that caught his attention. One concerned the death of five men in a landmine attack by the IRA near a BBC transmitter in Northern Ireland and the other highlighted a move by the Royal Albert Hall to ban a Frank Zappa concert that had been scheduled for later in the month. Different though they were, they raised the same query in his mind. What was it about human beings that made it impossible for them to coexist and find some sort of common ground?

Just asking the question left him feeling irritated, a mood that only increased as he tried unsuccessfully to stuff the newspaper into his coat pocket. His irritation gave way to a wry smile as realised why it wouldn't fit. That was where he'd put the small package that Mr McFadyen had given him earlier. He pulled it out and unwrapped it. It was a framed photograph of him standing arm in arm with Ma Smith. They were both smiling, obviously happy to be in each other's company. He ran his finger round the edge of the frame and absent-mindedly turned it over. There, in Ma's own handwriting, were the words, *My unexpected son* and the date: *Saturday 28th March 1964*. For a moment he wondered why she'd gone to the trouble of putting the details on the back. Then he remembered: that was the date the postman had delivered the letter containing the official confirmation of her guardianship.

He rewrapped the photograph as carefully as if it had been an ancient holy relic and put it back in his pocket. The café seemed oddly quiet as he got up and walked to the door, leaving the newspaper lying on the table. He no longer needed it to remind him of the inability of human beings just to live happily together. It was part of the mystery at the centre of his own life.

chapter 16
1981

Every time he'd relocated to another city, Matthew had travelled light. He carried little in the way of possessions, apart from his clothes and his portable typewriter, which fitted easily into the old Swiss Army rucksack he'd had for years. Once that was settled on his back, he'd pick up his record player in one hand and a cloth carrier bag containing his LP records in the other and head out of the door. That was all he needed to survive wherever he went. His most highly prized records were his Beatles albums. He couldn't contemplate a life in which he didn't regularly set *The White Album* or *Sgt Pepper* or *Abbey Road* on the turntable and sit down to listen to them one more time. Since the early 1960s they'd formed the soundtrack to his life. He knew the lyrics of every track by heart, he could sing along note-perfect with every lick and every guitar riff, and he had an encyclopaedic knowledge of The Beatles' discography. It was impossible for him to imagine any other popular music replacing them in his affections.

But one morning a couple of months after he'd returned to Manchester from Ma Smith's funeral, a new love entered his life. The sound emanating from the radio was unlike anything he'd heard before. It was loud and brash and in-your-face, with a walking bass line accented with guitar rhythms on the offbeat and coloured with strident interjections from a wind section of trumpet, trombone and saxophone. It fused elements of Caribbean calypso and reggae with English punk-rock and American rhythm and blues, and turned them into a musical concoction with an itchy restlessness you couldn't ignore and a rebellious energy that stopped you in your tracks. It was *Ska*. And it fixed itself in his mind for the rest of the day. That evening he went out and bought an album by The Specials, the Coventry band at the forefront of this reincarnation of a musical genre that had been born in 1950s Jamaica. He played it over and over again before he went to bed.

The obsessive side of his personality kicked in and over the next few months he bought every record The Specials had made and read up everything he could about them. Their music struck him as both a powerful cry of protest and a creative antidote to the bitter unrest and violence that was breaking out in cities across the country as a reaction to the unpopular policies of Margaret Thatcher's government. He went to hear them live as often as he could when they were within travelling distance of Manchester and found himself being drawn into the excitement of the audience, most of whom were a good ten years younger than he was.

That was where he first saw the unofficial uniform of the Ska bands and their devoted fans – the 'Rude Boys' and 'Rude Girls', as they chose to identify themselves. Like the music they loved, it was a brash hybrid of different styles, borrowing from the mod and skinhead fashions of the 1960s with a touch of Jamaican gangster style from a decade earlier. The girls wore either tight skirts with chequered tights or rockabilly swing dresses with white socks and high-heeled shoes. The boys, however, were the real fashionistas in their smart black suits, white shirts, preferably with button-down collars, and black skinny ties. Their drainpipe trousers were held up by black and white chequered braces and cut slightly short to show off their white socks and highly polished black brogues. And the really committed followers of the fashion finished everything off with a pair of wrap-around shades – worn even at night – and a pork-pie hat perched nattily on the head. It was a style that immediately appealed to Matthew. He envied the trendy young peacocks who strutted their stuff with such swagger and youthful abandon. But he'd been reminded often enough that he was too much of a geek to even begin to think of joining their number. His own wardrobe consisted of half a dozen shapeless T-shirts, a couple of well-worn jackets and sweaters, several pairs of jeans, and one long-out-of-fashion dark blue suit that he hadn't worn for years. He could only imagine what the guys at the supermarket where he was currently stacking shelves and manning the checkout would say if he arrived dressed like a mod. But it was, nonetheless, an image he couldn't get out of his mind.

It wasn't until he was struggling vainly one evening with yet another rewrite of his latest attempt at a detective novel that a thought occurred to him: maybe he was missing something, something that was staring him in the face; that picture that he had in his mind – the image of a

Ska-loving mod – might be just what he was looking for. He sat still for ten minutes, allowing his ideas to shape themselves into something he could work with. He'd take his inspiration from the edgy American crime fiction he'd been reading. And if he himself couldn't be like Philip Marlowe, then he'd create a character who, in literary terms at least, would be his late-twentieth-century grandchild.

When he thought he was ready, he ripped the half-filled page out of the typewriter and slipped a pristine sheet of white paper into the carriage. He'd use the racy first-person style of American detective fiction as his template again, but this time he'd do it with a character whose feet were firmly planted in the streets of an English city and whose ears were perfectly attuned to the music of 1980s rebellious youth culture. He began to type, slowly at first, then in a steady rhythm as the words and ideas began to flow:

It was three o'clock in the afternoon, the middle of June, and the sun was breaking through the clouds after a summer shower that had left the landscaped lawn I was walking past looking as bright and clear as a detail in a recently restored landscape by an Old Master. I was wearing my black suit, fresh from the cleaners, my favourite textured white shirt with the button-down collar, and a slim, dark tie. I was showing exactly an inch of white sock below the bottoms of my well-tailored straight-leg trousers. The black leather brogues on my feet looked expensive. *They were expensive!* I don't mind you knowing that with my wrap-around shades and pork-pie hat I felt more than a match for anything that could happen. But that's no more than you'd expect from a mod who could dance most of the night to a heavy Ska rhythm and still be wide awake and on the job before lunchtime the next day. I needed to look my best. I was about to shake hands with more money than I'd ever dreamed of.

He read through his first paragraph. It wasn't bad. He'd go through it again in the morning. But it was encouraging enough for him to start typing again, even more confidently this time:

The steps up to the front door of the house were as white and regular as a movie star's teeth after ten sessions with an orthodontist whose prices meant he could afford to have a spare Rolls-Royce in the garage. They were so perfect I thought I might be the first person ever to have stood on them. I pressed the bell and checked my reflection in the stained glass of the tall window beside the door while I waited. Whoever was supposed to be answering took so long that I'd time to give my brogues an extra polish by rubbing them on the backs of my trousers. I didn't mind the delay. This was the first time my services as a private detective had been called for by any of the country set. I wanted to get it right.

The door was opened by a maid dressed like the waitresses in a fancy tearoom I'd once been taken to by a grateful client whose guilty secrets

I'd managed to keep just the way he wanted them – secret, that is. She showed me into a room with panelled walls and plush velvet chairs and invited me to take a seat. She had blue eyes with eyelids that fluttered like butterflies when they've been disturbed by an unexpected breeze. I'd seen this happen with girls I'd met before. I knew she liked me.

My thoughts about the girl were suddenly arrested when the oak panelling on the opposite side of the room began to break away from the wall. I wondered for a second if the house might actually be slowly disintegrating. It wasn't. It was a door cleverly disguised as part of the wall to conceal it from city boys like me. I was pretty sure that anyone who'd been here before me and who came from the streets where I was raised hadn't waited to be formally admitted. Unlike me on this occasion, they must have come for purely nefarious purposes. I let that thought go and kept my attention on what was happening. This wasn't my natural environment and I had to stay alert.

The door in the wall creaked as it opened wider and an elderly man shuffled into the room dragging his left leg behind him as if it wasn't properly attached to him any longer. It was summer and I was hot and beginning to sweat, but he was wearing a heavy brown tweed suit made from a cloth that looked as rough as heavy-duty sandpaper. He had the tired and supercilious expression that made me think he'd been educated at an elite public school, that he probably still had plenty of money left in the bank, but definitely not much life left in him.

'I'm Sir Ronald Ross,' he said in a weak, gasping, husky voice that reminded me of the noise a kettle makes just before it starts to boil. For some reason he looked ·dubiously at my smart attire as he reached forward to shake my hand. 'Are you the man I've been recommended to speak to?'

Matthew paused again. It was time for his Ska-loving, sharp-dressing, smart-talking, streetwise creation to introduce himself. But he hadn't thought of what to call him! And he knew instinctively that getting the name right would be crucial. He got up from the typewriter to make a cup of tea and give himself time to think. The tin where he kept the tea was empty, but fortunately he'd bought a new box of teabags on his way home earlier in the day. It was only when he started to open it that he realised, to his annoyance, that he'd picked up a box of Earl Grey tea at the supermarket rather than the normal English Breakfast variety he always drank. It was too late to go back and change it. And, anyway, he didn't want to stop writing when he was just getting into a rhythm. He didn't much like the smell of it when he poured the boiling water over it, but it would have to do. To make things worse, when he went to the fridge, he discovered that he'd run out of milk. Drinking tea without milk was not something that he'd ever understood and certainly not something he'd ever done. Well, there was a first time for everything. He picked up his cup and sat down at the typewriter again.

Now, what to call his character? His first thought was that Johnny would do for his first name. It was informal, laid-back. Then he tried linking that with a variety of surnames and eventually plumped for Johnny Bright. That had the right ring to it for a detective who was young, clever and streetwise, who would be willing to bend the rules if necessary, but who· was essentially clean and trustworthy. When he typed it onto the page, however, it didn't look right. Too neat, too easy, too *obvious*. He got up again and paced round the room with his cup of tea in his hand. Actually, he thought, this tea wasn't that bad. It was different. Maybe he could get to like it, become a different kind of Matthew Gold...

That brought a cynical smile to his face. He looked around the shabby room and thought about his current prospects. He was heading nowhere. It was the same old, same old. But a different kind of Matthew Gold? A new Matthew Gold? Dream on! But it was a thought that set his ideas going in a new direction. His hero, he admitted to himself, had to be, at least to some extent, an extension of himself. Better still, he had to be the opposite of who he was. Everything he wished he could be. A kind of alter ego. He smiled to himself again and this time there was no hint of cynicism in his expression. If he felt anything, it was a surge of excitement that he might be on the verge of creating a character with a credibility and vitality that would bring him to life in the minds of readers. Or, at the very least, convince a publisher that it was worth letting him loose in print.

A new Matthew Gold? Ignoring the typewriter, he reached over for his notepad that he used to quickly scribble down ideas that came to him. He sat for a minute with his pen in hand, poised to write, waiting for just the right words. Then he wrote very deliberately in bold capital letters: THE OPPOSITE OF MATTHEW GOLD = MONTY SILVER. He pushed his notepad and pen aside and began to type again.

I stood up, looked him in the eye and shook his hand firmly.

'I'm Monty Silver, chief investigator of the Sterling Detective Agency. And yes, I am the man your lawyer, Virgil Nevis, recommended to you. How can I be of service to you, Sir Ronald?'

'You're not what I expected, but Virgil spoke highly of you and I need to trust someone. Let's sit down and I'll tell you what I'm so concerned about.'

He summoned the maid, who came back into the room carrying a silver tray with a pot of Earl Grey tea. She set out two cups and saucers of such delicate bone china that I wondered if they might dissolve when she poured in the tea.

'Is Earl Grey alright for you, Mr Silver?' He asked the question with a contemptuous edge that reduced his already breathy voice to a snake-like hiss. 'Perhaps you're used to something more ordinary. English Breakfast?'

I assured him that I was more than happy with the variety of tea the maid was serving and eager to hear why he'd sent for me.

'It's my granddaughter. She went up to Oxford last September to study Classics. She hasn't come home or even contacted the family since the end of term.'

'Maybe she's just decided to go off somewhere for a few weeks,' I suggested, holding my cup in front of me as I spoke to let him see that I'd drunk more than half of my tea. 'She's young and there's a lot of great music to be heard over the summer.'

He shook his head and leaned forward, his voice dropping to a husky whisper even though there wasn't anyone else in the room to overhear what he was saying.

'We're worried about her. We're Church of England, of course, but she's fallen in with a Catholic priest at university – a good-looking young fellow, by all accounts. She talks about him a lot. Been spending a lot of time with him, as far as we can tell. We've checked with his superiors and it seems he's gone missing too. The whole thing is troubling. And we don't want it to get out to the newspapers. My son's an MP. Real prospects of getting a cabinet post at the next reshuffle. Any kind of scandal in the press wouldn't help him at all. We need someone to make discreet enquiries, Mr Silver. Can you do it?'

For the third time that evening Matthew smiled to himself. He was pleased with the start he'd made. He'd set the story up nicely. Tomorrow morning he was on the early shift and that meant getting up at half past five. It was time to get to bed. He'd sleep on it, let it tick over in his mind throughout the day, and start writing again when he got home from work in the afternoon. Maybe there was still hope that he could be a published writer...

chapter 17
1982

It was eleven o'clock on a pleasant but otherwise unremarkable Friday morning in the middle of September and Matthew Gold was savouring his Earl Grey tea with just a slice of lemon. There was more than one reason for persisting with his recently acquired taste. Not only had he quickly learned to enjoy the flavour, but it also saved money on milk. In a couple of hours he'd be leaving for a two o'clock start at the supermarket and he knew he ought to sit down at the typewriter and get something done on the latest manuscript he was trying to complete. The truth was he'd almost completely lost heart. It was just over eighteen months since he'd returned to Manchester from Ma Smith's funeral, almost twelve months since he'd completed his first attempt at a novel with Monty Silver as his central character, and exactly three months since he'd hand-delivered it to Crimezone Mysteries. The girl in the dreary office on the fifth floor of a nondescript building at the end of Deansgate in Manchester had told him that she'd personally make sure it got to her boss. He would certainly take a look at it and get back to him, she promised, though she couldn't say precisely when that would be. She didn't look much older than sixteen or seventeen and he didn't have much faith in her confident-sounding assurances.

Having already received nine out-of-hand rejections from better-known publishers to whom he'd mailed the book, Crimezone Mysteries, of whom he knew next to nothing, was something of a desperate last measure. As the days and weeks passed with no word from them, he became more and more despondent. His hopes, which had had been raised in the excitement of creating his Ska-loving detective, looked set to be dashed yet again. And the whole thing was beginning to get to him. His stammer had been getting worse for the last few weeks, and that was always a sure sign that he was under stress. He'd give it another month, he told himself, and if he didn't hear anything in that time, he'd draw a fat red line under the writing thing and find something else, *something useful* to do with his life.

He was about to force himself to sit down and try to write something – *anything* – when the doorbell rang. He made his way downstairs to the street-level door by the side of the launderette. He always seemed to end up living above a launderette! Most people didn't even realise that the door led to an upstairs flat, which meant that he had few callers. Wondering who it might be, but grateful for an excuse to put off getting on with what he knew he ought to be doing, he prepared himself to be confronted by someone with a clothes-filled plastic bag trying to find their way into the launderette. He was surprised to see a tall, lanky young man holding a brown leather briefcase and dressed in a smart pinstriped business suit that would have looked old fogeyish and unnecessarily formal on a sunny day even on a man twice his age. His tousled, wavy blond hair and youthful grin were amusingly at odds with his clothes. Matthew was even more surprised to see the teenage girl he'd met briefly at the office of Crimezone Mysteries three months earlier standing by the side of his unexpected and unknown visitor. Her spiky hair was exactly the same colour as that of her male companion. Her dress, however, reflected an altogether different fashion sense to his. The studded leather jacket, ripped jeans, loose-fitting T-shirt emblazoned with the name of a local band, and heavy-duty boots announced unambiguously that she was firmly in the middle of a somewhat belated punk phase.

He looked from one to the other, with no idea of how he should greet the unlikely couple standing in front of him or why they were on his doorstep. His caller had no such hesitation in speaking.

'Am I correct in assuming that I'm addressing Mr Matthew Gold?' he asked with a quizzical expression that combined with his grin in a way that made it impossible for Matthew not to smile back at him. 'I do hope so. I really need to talk to him.'

'Yyyes, I'm Mmmatthew G-G-Gold,' he replied. His smile gave way to a flush of embarrassment as he struggled yet again to tell a stranger his name.

The young man didn't seem to notice.

'Excellent, excellent!' He seemed genuinely pleased to have found the person he was looking for and immediately pressed on with his mission.

'May we come in, please? I'm Julian Barrington-Williams and this is my sister, Emmeline. Our friends call me Jools and her Emm. And when they want to refer to both of us, they call us the BWs. Feel free to do the same. I run Crimezone Mysteries and when she's not away at school, Emm helps me with a bit of admin and by reading some of the stuff we get in. I want to talk to you about your manuscript. Great title, by the way: *The Priest and the Princess*. I really like that.'

Matthew led the way up the stairs, trying as they went to apologise to his visitors for the messy state of the flat. From their lack of any kind of reaction it was clear that they either didn't notice or didn't care about such bourgeois conventions as tidiness and order. They were, however, delighted to learn that he had Earl Grey tea in his kitchen and readily accepted his invitation to share some. Neither of them seemed in the least perturbed by having it served in chipped mugs or by the fact that there weren't proper chairs for them to sit on. Emmeline sat cross-legged on the floor while her brother settled himself beside Matthew on the edge of his bed. This ought to feel awkward, he thought, but there was something about this unusual brother and sister that made him feel surprisingly at ease.

Julian Barrington-Williams pulled Matthew's manuscript from his briefcase and began to explain more fully the reason for their surprise visit.

'My family has been in the publishing business for four generations. You've probably heard of Barrwill Press. We publish a lot of well-known writers. All kinds of stuff – fiction, travel journals, academic treatises, classy coffee-table books – you name it, we do it. The trouble is, I'm not terribly comfortable in that environment. It might be OK if I was forty years older. But I'm still in my twenties and it's all a bit too stuffy and well established for my liking. I want to do something more exciting, take a risk, do something a bit more cutting edge. My father's so fed up with me badgering him that he's given in. So six months ago he gave me three years and a reasonable amount of cash to try to set up my own thing. I'm particularly interested in crime fiction and, to be honest, Barrwill Press regard that as a bit beneath them. I've got a point to prove to the old man.'

It had always struck Matthew as a ridiculous statement whenever he heard people talk about having to pinch themselves to make sure they weren't dreaming. Now, for the first time in his life, he could understand what they meant. After all these years of unsuccessfully trying to get his stuff published, after all the agonising months spent waiting and hoping for a reply that never came, after all the demoralising, curt rejection letters, a man with a genuine interest in the kind of stuff he wanted to write and enough money to set up a publishing company turns up at the door making complimentary remarks about his work. He didn't pinch himself. But he put his hand on Julian Barrington-Williams' arm and took a long, slow breath.

'And you think that mmmy mmmanuscript is g-g-good enough fffor you to p-p-publish?'

'I don't *think*. I *know*. We want to publish you. As I said, I really like your writing. And so does Emm. I've been on the road for a bit, so she read your manuscript before I did. She's been nagging me to read it ever since. And I'm glad I did. I read it at one sitting. You've captured the essence of classic 1930s American crime fiction and set it in 1980s Britain with a character who's unmistakably part of the culture on this side of the Atlantic. It's what I've been looking for. Let me tell you how we work and you can say if you'd be comfortable being part of it.'

For the next twenty minutes Julian Barrington-Williams talked excitedly about his philosophy of publishing. His motto, he explained, was *Find the Writers, Focus on the Readers*. His experience with Barrwill Press meant that he had useful contacts in the business. But rather than spending all his time schmoozing his peers and persuading the trade magazines to pick up a press release, he wanted to invest his energy and resources in developing a tight-knit group of writers and then cultivating a relationship with their readers.

His passion was infectious and Matthew found himself being swept along by his enthusiasm. Years of disappointment, however, had made him cautious, wary of glib promises and clever sales talk. But what had he to lose? If he signed up with Crimezone Mysteries and nothing came of it, he'd be no worse off than he was at present. He might even have agreed there and then had Emmeline Barrington-Williams not interrupted her brother in mid-sentence before turning to Matthew.

'I need to apologise for my brother,' she laughed. 'He's a very persuasive talker when an idea gets hold of him. I have to slow him down sometimes and remind him that other people need time to catch up. Why don't we give you the weekend to think about this? Maybe we could take you out for a meal next week and take it a bit further. What do you think?'

Matthew, who was struggling to process everything he was hearing, was grateful for her intervention and he readily agreed to her proposal to meet the following week when he had a day off work. He shook hands with his visitors at the bottom of the stairs and watched them cross the road and get into a silver-grey sports car, hardly able to believe what had happened. He remounted the stairs and got ready to leave for work. His head was buzzing with questions. Had his luck really turned? Was Julian Barrington-Williams and his offer for real? Was it possible that, after all this time, he was about to become a published author?

He managed to get through his shift without his mind ever being fully on what he was doing. Customers came and went and the minutes ticked slowly by. But all he could think of was the conversation with the BWs earlier in the day. He was relieved when it was time to clock out. It was getting on for eleven o'clock that night when he sat down to eat the takeaway chicken curry he'd picked up on the way home. And he was still half-afraid that what had happened twelve hours earlier had been just a dream.

chapter 18
1982

Shortly before twelve o'clock on the Wednesday after the unexpected visit of Julian and Emmeline Barrington-Williams to his flat, Matthew Gold was walking a little nervously into the appropriately named Writers' Meeting House, one of Manchester's most expensive and exclusive restaurants. He wasn't sure if his ten-year-old suit, which he'd got back from the dry-cleaners just a couple of hours earlier, would be smart enough for such a place, and his usual concern at the prospect of having to speak to a relative stranger in an unfamiliar setting served only to compound his growing anxiety. He needn't have worried. The maître d' who greeted him on entry had clearly been primed to look out for him and immediately put him at his ease. Matthew suspected that his unflappable and courteous manner was not simply a result of his professional expertise, but that he'd been forewarned to be extra patient with a guest who might look a little out of place in such a high-end establishment and who might well have difficulty in saying his own name.

'Ah yes, Mr Gold,' he said genially when Matthew had eventually managed to identify himself. 'You're a guest of the BWs. They're regular patrons, good friends of ours. Follow me, please.'

He ushered him through the crowded main dining area to a private room where brother and sister were already seated at a round table with places elaborately set for three on an immaculate white linen tablecloth. They were both dressed as they had been when Matthew had met them a few days before – Julian in his pinstriped suit and Emmeline in her punk garb – and they were clearly completely at ease, notwithstanding Emmeline's incongruous dress, in such an upmarket establishment. It was Emmeline who spoke first.

'Thank you, Edward,' she said, addressing the maître d' before getting up and taking Matthew by surprise with an affectionate hug. 'It's good to see you again. We're really hoping we can tie some things down after lunch. But it's always better to do business after a good meal. So let's eat first and then we can talk. We've asked Edward just to bring us a selection of whatever's best on the menu at the moment. It'll give you a chance to sample our favourite restaurant in town.'

The seclusion of the tastefully decorated room in which they were meeting and the easy flow of their conversation with the attentive waiter indicated beyond any doubt to Matthew that the BWs, as he called them, were indeed regular and valued patrons. And that was borne out by what followed – a dazzling array of courses accompanied by a bottle of fine wine that wouldn't have disappointed the most demanding gourmet. To Matthew, whose usual fare for the last sixteen years had consisted of takeaway meals from inexpensive fast-food establishments located in the less salubrious areas of the city, it was a banquet fit for royalty. While his two fellow diners chatted happily as they ate, he was intent on savouring the gastronomic delights and focusing on using the right cutlery in the right order. Developing a taste for Earl Grey tea was one thing: a simple pleasure in itself, but a significant step in his growing realisation that his life had been constrained by the social class and limited circumstances into which he'd been born. The world, he was learning, was full of good things he had yet to discover. To savour food like this, however, in a restaurant of this quality, was to experience for the first time what luxuries and indulgences money could buy. And it stirred in him an envy of what others possessed and a longing for what he didn't yet have.

When the meal was over and the table was cleared, the maître d' set up coffee and, to Matthew's relief, a pot of Earl Grey tea. Emmeline laid out a wodge of typed papers she'd pulled from her brother's briefcase.

'He does the big-picture stuff,' she explained with a glance towards her brother. 'But I look after the details or we might never actually get things done.'

'Just be glad I let you be part of what I'm doing,' her brother countered with a knowing look. 'If I don't keep you busy, Dad might send you back to finish your studies at that school you hate so much.'

Matthew joined in their laughter. But his was a forced laugh that served as a cover for what he was really feeling. Their easy-going relationship provoked questions he'd always tried to shut out of his mind. How different might his life have been – how different might *he* have been – if he'd had a brother or sister? Or if he'd had normal parents, like other kids? That moment, sitting there observing the dynamics of their sibling relationship and enjoying the benefits of their inherited wealth, seemed to encapsulate what he'd known all his life. He was an outsider, a loner, an observer. He was looking in at life, and he wanted desperately to be part of it.

'Penny for your thoughts, Matthew.' Emmeline's voice broke into his musing.

'Nnnothing really,' he answered. 'J-j-just thinking ab-about what wwwe're going to d-d-discuss.'

'Well, then, let's get on with it.' Julian pulled two pens from the inside pocket of his jacket and laid them side by side on the table. 'Let me pour coffee. You do the tea, Emm, and then we can talk business.'

Matthew was aware that his heart was beating faster and he reminded himself to follow Grampa's advice: let yourself relax and breathe slowly whenever you're excited or anxious. This was what he'd dreamed of, a moment he'd feared would never come. He tried to assume what he hoped was a matter-of-fact expression as Julian began to outline his offer.

'Like I told you last week, we really like your manuscript. It's what I've been looking for. And what's more, I think you've definitely got more than one book in you. Now, I know there's a solid audience out there for crime fiction. But I also know that we need to refresh the genre if we want to attract and build a younger readership. Your guy, Monty Silver, could be just what we need to do that. We want to publish in paperback, of course. But instead of 8 per cent royalties – which is what most publishers offer authors on paperbacks – we're willing to make that 10 per cent. We'll also give you an upfront payment of £1,000. And, if you'll sign up with us for another four Monty Silver mysteries over the next few years, we'll give you a retainer of £1,500 a year. Then, providing everything goes well and sales are high, and if you're happy and we're happy, we'll look at our agreement again at the end of the two years.' He leaned back in his chair, folded his arms and asked, 'How does that sound to you so far?'

Matthew tried to look as if he was reviewing the offer. What he was really thinking was that this was an offer he couldn't refuse. If it all worked out, he could give up his job at the supermarket, find a better place to live and concentrate fully on writing.

'It sssounds g-g-good to me,' was all he managed by way of reply.

'Excellent, excellent.' Julian patted his hand on the papers lying on the table in front of him. 'But before we sign anything, I need to be honest with you. There's a couple of things we've written into the deal that we think will be good for both parties, for you as the author and us as the publisher.'

Matthew's heart sank. The elation he'd been feeling was quickly swept away by an overwhelming fear of what Julian might be about to say. Surely it wasn't all about to be snatched away from him before it had even begun. He took long, slow breaths and prepared himself for whatever he was about to hear.

'There are two things. First, I think the name Matthew Gold would look... well, too formal on the cover of a paperback crime novel. Sounds a bit like your geography teacher's name. Let's shorten it to Matt Gee. That's sharper, to the point. It's got the right ring about it.'

Matthew couldn't think of any reason to be unhappy about the suggested pen name. Now, however, he noticed that Julian was speaking more slowly and watching him closely to gauge his reaction.

'Then there's the matter of how we publicise your book. Normally I'd want to get a newly signed author doing interviews, big them up with the press, that kind of thing. Especially as we're trying to get to a younger readership. Forgive me for being personal, but even from our two meetings so far, I suspect you might find that kind of early exposure to press interviews stressful. So here's my thinking. Let's protect you from that. It needn't be a negative if we're smart enough to use it to our advantage. If the first book gets the reception we hope and expect and we start to get requests for interviews, then we can begin to create an impression of you as not only the writer of mysteries, but as something of a mystery man yourself, someone who wants his true identity to be a secret. Drop hints that you're something of a recluse, or that you've got a secret you want to keep hidden – something like that. We can throw them a few red herrings, set them on a few false trails. And that leaves you free to concentrate on your writing.'

The room was silent as Julian and Emmeline waited and watched for Matthew's response. They didn't have to wait long for the silence to be broken by a long, slow sigh of relief from Matthew.

'That wwwould be g-g-great,' he said. 'All I wwwant to do is write. G-g-give mmme the p-p-pen and I'll sign rrright now.'

Julian was already unscrewing the top off one of the pens when his sister put her hand on his and stopped him in his tracks.

'Not so fast,' she laughed as she tucked the document into an envelope she pulled out from the bottom of the pile. 'You need to read through it carefully, Matthew. It's a fairly standard contract, but you might want to get someone who knows about these things to check it out before you sign. Make sure my eager brother isn't trying to fleece you.'

He nodded his agreement and took the envelope from her. At the suggestion of Julian, whose confidence in getting Matthew's signature on the contract didn't waver, they drank a toast to their future partnership.

'To Matt Gee and Monty Silver,' Emmeline proposed, raising her glass aloft. 'May they solve many a mystery… and earn us all a bit of money.'

It was gone three o'clock by the time they left the room and walked through the now deserted main restaurant together. Edward shook hands with them and asked if they'd had a good lunch. They assured him that it had not only been good but also unusually productive and potentially profitable. Julian and Emmeline were still chatting with him as Matthew excused himself and walked back onto the street. He folded the envelope he'd been given and tucked it into the inside pocket of his jacket, threw back his shoulders, and strode confidently along. It had been a lunch that he hoped would change his life.

chapter 19
1988

The bright red Merlin TF two-seater sports car pulled out of the driveway on a Saturday morning and gave a satisfying roar as the driver pressed firmly on the accelerator pedal and drove at more than the legal speed through the newly built housing estate on the outskirts of Manchester. Many of the houses were still in the final stages of completion, but the residents of those that were already occupied, even if they hadn't yet opened their windows, would have heard more than the revving of the engine as their neighbour sped proudly by in his latest acquisition. August had been unusually wet, even for the north-west of England, but at last the weather had taken a turn for the better and the man at the wheel had retracted the roof of his convertible to feel the warmth of the sun and allow everyone else to enjoy the sounds coming from the expensive upgrade he'd had fitted before taking delivery of his car – a high-spec, top-of the-range, very loud sound system. And those who were knowledgeable about such things would have recognised immediately from the heavy walking bass and the tch-tch-tch of the rhythm guitar on the off-beat that this particular motorist had a passion for Ska as well as a taste for fast cars. The trendy magazines might be confidently announcing that the boom for this particular musical genre was over, but for him it had become a lifelong love affair that would endure long after fashions in popular music had moved on.

Matthew Gold was a happy man, pleased with himself and pleased with life in general. His new house and new car were just the two most obvious material possessions that proclaimed his status as a successful writer. His relationship with Crimezone Mysteries had worked out better than even the entrepreneurial Julian or the ever-optimistic Emmeline Barrington-Williams had imagined. Six years and six novels after their first encounter, he was on his way to meet them and sign yet another extension to his initial two-year contract. He reached for the cassette player, ejected the tape of The Specials that was playing, and replaced it with one that was lying conveniently on the passenger seat beside him. He'd already played it more than a dozen times since he'd recorded it from the radio less than a month before, but it never failed to give him a buzz of satisfaction.

He fast-forwarded the tape of a recent radio arts programme to the point where the ten-minute piece on his writing began. The presenter focused first on the niche in the market that Crimezone Mysteries had carved out for itself with its team of exciting young and previously unknown writers. But very quickly he moved on to feature what he described as 'the jewel in their crown, the Monty Silver Mysteries by Matt Gee'. He listed the six books in order of their publication – *The Priest and the Princess; The*

Case of the Missing Professor; The Boys in the Band; Who Killed Mr Grey?; Death at the Freshers' Ball and *The Poisoning of Mary Morrison* – commenting favourably on each of them before summing up with a paragraph that Matthew had replayed so many times that he could recite along with him:

> It's no exaggeration to say that Matt Gee – whoever this mysterious writer is – has created a character who really does rival Philip Marlowe for a place in the pantheon of unforgettable sleuths who perfectly fit with their time and place. The Ska-loving, mod-dressing Monty Silver does for Britain in the 1980s what Raymond Chandler's hip-talking gumshoe did for America in the 1930s. And Gee is churning out these novels at a rate that would have made his esteemed predecessor gasp in astonishment. His growing number of fans and his grateful publisher will hope that the flow continues without abating or losing its edge.

Matthew ran the tape back and let it play one more time. He loved that phrase: 'Matt Gee – whoever this mysterious writer is…' The publicity had worked a treat. In Julian's own words, he'd 'played the popular press like a violin'. They'd fallen for his seemingly off-the-cuff but carefully scripted and rehearsed remarks about the reclusive lifestyle and unusual personality of his most successful writer. The bogus clues he'd fed them about who this mysterious literary figure might be had led to wide-ranging speculation as to his true identity. It had caught the public imagination to the point where it had become something of a running national joke, figuring in the routines of more than one television comic. One opposition MP, annoyed at the Prime Minister's absence from the house during a debate he considered to be of major importance, had even suggested that she was 'becoming as elusive as Matt Gee'.

He would often laugh with Julian and Emmeline at the stunt they'd pulled and the way in which Matt Gee had infiltrated the nation's consciousness. But the irony that he chose to ignore was that Matt Gee had wormed his way just as successfully into *his* life. Without fully realising what was happening, he'd begun to model himself on what he imagined Matt Gee to be like. No longer was he just the illegitimate son of a teenage mother who'd died in childbirth, the child with the stammer from the miners' rows in Bellmill, the university dropout having to settle for a series of dead-end jobs, the person who brought bad luck and even death to everyone who got close to him. His birth certificate might give his name as Matthew Gold. It was a secret known only to a handful of people, but *he was Matt Gee and he would live like Matt Gee*. For the first time in his life he had money and he wasn't about to apologise for that. After all he'd been through, he reckoned he deserved his success and he was determined to enjoy the pleasures that came with it. Gone were the baggy T-shirts and scruffy jeans of what he described to himself as his 'years in poverty and obscurity', to be replaced by his yuppy look – Oxford shirts, khaki trousers and loafers and, on a day like today, a pair of expensive Aviator sunglasses. He'd even toyed from time to time with adopting a mod look in deference to his love of Ska, but he took one look at himself in the mirror and decided he looked so ridiculous that it would be better to leave that to his fictional creation. He'd settle for dressing like Matt Gee.

But if his nom de plume provided him with a handy template on which to pattern his lifestyle, his literary creation offered him something even more desirable, something that mattered more than clothes or possessions, something that went right to his soul. Monty Silver was *everything* that Matthew Gold longed to be. Monty Silver knew his place in the universe and the part he was created to play; Monty Silver was the master of repartee; Monty Silver was always in command of the situation; Monty Silver always got the most attractive girl; Monty Silver always found the answers, uncovered the truths, and solved the mysteries; Monty Silver was always on the side of right, always ensured that good triumphed over evil and that justice was done in the end. The only problem was that in those times when bad dreams disturbed Matthew's sleep and he woke in the middle of the night, he knew that he was nothing like that.

By the time he turned into the tree-lined avenue leading to the Old Rectory Hotel, the tape had ended and he could put such troubling thoughts out of his mind and slip back into the role of the successful crime writer without a care in the world. The venue, three miles outside Wilmound and a little downmarket from the places where they usually met, had been chosen by the BWs for the protection they felt it offered from the possible attentions of the media. Just to be doubly sure of avoiding prying eyes, they'd told him to drive through the main parking area and leave his car under the trees behind the hotel. He wasn't sure why they were so anxious not to be seen, but he was happy to go along with what they'd suggested.

He entered the hotel by a back door where Emmeline met him. She took him by the arm, leading him through the kitchens and into a comfortable but unpretentious room where Julian was sitting at a table with two other men, neither of whom Matthew recognised. He couldn't think why anyone else would be present when he was renewing his contract with Crimezone Mysteries. Nor could he understand why they would risk letting people he didn't know in on the closely guarded secret of his identity. He looked questioningly at Julian, who recognised his obvious confusion.

'Don't worry, Matthew,' he said reassuringly. 'We *are* going to do your contract. And don't worry about our secret. It's as safe as ever with these guys. But there's something we need to talk about. Something I've been working on for a few months now. I didn't want to say anything about it until I was sure we could get it over the line. First, let me introduce Nick Grant and Rod Mason.'

The two men stood up and shook hands with him and he tried to react as naturally as possible, though he was still completely nonplussed by their presence. At that point, Emmeline, who'd slipped out of the room after getting him to the door, returned carrying a tray of tea and coffee and biscuits. Her intervention allowed the tension to ease and by the time they'd taken their places around the table and filled their cups, Julian was ready to enlighten him more fully on the situation.

'Nick and Rod head up their own production company and they've approached me about the prospect of adapting your novels for a TV series. I'll let Rod explain their thinking and what they've got in mind.'

Matthew had sometimes wondered if his books could be dramatised and serialised, but it had always seemed too much to hope for. His hitherto puzzled expression changed instantly. His face lit up and his eyes widened as Julian's words registered. The others in the room couldn't help but laugh at his obvious delight at the prospect. When the laughter died down Rod Mason leaned on the table and began to speak.

'Matthew, your books are something of a publishing phenomenon. They've created huge interest, but inevitably there's still a lot of folk who've not yet read them. And your stories have got mass appeal. There's another market to be cracked. And you'll be aware that ITV have been running a dramatisation of the Philip Marlowe stories they've bought in from the States. I think the time is ripe for us to get Monty Silver on television. Nick's already been thinking about just how we could pitch this…'

'Yes, I've been giving it a lot of thought,' Nick Grant interjected. 'There are two crime dramas that I've always thought were a cut above the rest. There's *Morse*, which has something of a middle to highbrow feel to it with its literary allusions and its references to classical music. Then there was *Shoestring*, with a detective who was much younger than Inspector Morse – a computer expert who'd had a breakdown and launched his investigations from his show on local radio. I think the premise stretched credibility a bit too far, but it seemed to work. Got decent viewing figures…'

'There's a gap between those two shows,' Rod Mason picked up again. 'And we think that the *Monty Silver Mysteries* would fill that space. Like your books, it would pull in a younger audience. And it would transfer well to television. It's got music, contemporary setting, a detective who's different. We've lined up a really good scriptwriter who's well practised at adapting books for the small screen. If we can get the right actor to play Monty Silver – and we've got somebody very much in mind – I think we could have a character to rival Arthur Daley in the public imagination.'

The room was silent for a moment and four pairs of eyes stared at Matthew Gold, watching and waiting for his response. He looked back at each of them in turn and still said nothing. Then his face broke into a broad grin.

'I think it's a g-g-great idea,' he said, punching his right fist into his left hand repeatedly. Four other pairs of hands responded with a round of applause.

'Right,' said Julian, 'that's settled. We'll get the legal guys to draw up the necessary documents and we can get on with it.'

They shook hands all round and the two men left the room. Matthew signed the contracts that Emmeline set in front of him, though after the conversation they'd just had, that seemed like an anticlimax. Even greater success now beckoned to him. He looked again at the brother and sister who'd brought about such a transformation in his life. His relationship with them was more than just professional. They genuinely seemed to care about him and they'd become his friends. Really the only reasonably close friends he had. Of course, he'd made other acquaintances in the city, people who shared his interests and with whom he met up with from time to time. There had been a number of women with whom he'd had brief and intensely physical and passionate relationships. But nothing that lasted, nothing that had the potential to develop into a loving lifelong partnership. No matter. He had his writing. He had created a character who might soon be stepping off the page and on to the nation's television screens. And he had Matt Gee – not just a nom de plume, more like a secret friend in whose company he could walk. And that would be enough. That would have to be enough.

chapter 20
1996

The ballroom of the Petram Hotel in London's West End was crowded for the Annual Dinner and Awards Ceremony of the Companions of Sherlock Society. As had been the rule for the nearly seventy years the society had been in existence, the event was taking place on 6th January, the date popularly believed by devotees of the Sherlock Holmes stories to be the birthday of Baker Street's entirely fictional but most famous resident. Membership of this prestigious club was by invitation only and consisted almost exclusively of writers of detective fiction. To be initiated into its ranks was a mark of the respect an author was held in by their peers and was an honour highly prized by any practitioner of the craft. But to be the recipient of one of its awards was the ultimate accolade to which anyone who followed in the footsteps of Sir Arthur Conan Doyle could aspire.

It had been a miserably wet and blustery day in London, but no one fortunate enough to have a place at one of the tables would have missed the occasion even if the capital had been hit by a tornado. Whether by accident or because a senior member of the organising committee with an eye to publicity had leaked it, word had got out to the press and media that the main award of the evening, the Crime Writer of the Decade, would be presented to the writer of the *Monty Silver Mysteries*. In itself that might have aroused enough interest to have crept into the inside pages of one of the Sunday broadsheets. But since it inevitably implied that the true identity of Matt Gee would be revealed, interest in the goings-on of the Companions of Sherlock Society was, if not quite at fever pitch, certainly higher than anyone could remember in the last fifty years. Requests for press passes to the event had swelled to three times their usual number and, for the first time ever, a television news crew was to be admitted.

Julian and Emmeline Barrington-Williams pulled up in a black limousine at a back entrance to the hotel half an hour before the rest of the guests were due to arrive. They were ushered discreetly into an anteroom behind the stage at the front of the ballroom. Between them they were supporting an elderly man whose shoulders were stooped and who appeared to have considerable difficulty in walking. His coat collar was turned up, obscuring most of his face, and his large fedora hat, which looked to be a couple of sizes too large, was pulled down over his eyes. As soon as they entered the room and the door was closed, the elderly man straightened up, threw off his coat, and hung his hat on a hook on the wall.

'I hope I'm a b-b-better writer than I am an actor,' he laughed. 'And at l-l-least I won't ever have to d-d-do that again.'

His two companions laughed with him, but Matthew Gold's was a nervous laugh that betrayed his anxiety at what was about to happen later in the evening. When they'd first been informed of the award some three months earlier, Julian and Emmeline had felt immediately that this was the right time to end the subterfuge that they'd maintained successfully and profitably for fourteen years. Matthew had initially been more reticent about revealing his identity. The value he placed on his privacy and his fear of the requests for interviews that might flood in were uppermost in his thoughts. In the end, however, they'd persuaded him that the media attention would give another boost to book sales and keep him right at the forefront of people's minds when they walked into a bookstore. More importantly, they insisted, he'd now get the recognition he deserved. Their ruse had served them well, but it was time for the world to know who Matt Gee really was.

As he'd continued to think about it in the succeeding weeks, he even began to look forward to the recognition that would come his way: Matthew Gold, the boy from the miners' rows made good, the kid with the stammer who'd learned how to use words to tell stories and solve mysteries. People would now know who he was and what he'd become. But his feelings still swung between anticipation and trepidation. He kept remembering a conversation he'd overheard between two women in a tea shop one day, one of whom had a large birthmark on the left side of her face. She was describing to her friend how she'd felt when she decided to stop applying the heavy make-up she'd always used to disguise the vivid red mark on her cheek. She'd been nervous about doing it, and she knew that some people would stare and a few might even make unkind remarks.

'But this,' she said defiantly, pointing to the blemish, 'this is part of me, part of who I am. And I knew that until I faced the world with that truth, I'd never be free to be myself.'

He wished then that he'd had the guts to butt in, to apologise for overhearing their conversation, to tell her about his stammer, to ask her how she found the courage and how she'd felt the first time she'd gone out without her make-up. Over the last three months he'd gone back to the same tea shop several times hoping to see her, determined to pluck up the courage to approach her, but he never saw her again.

The buzz of chatter coming from the ballroom alerted them to the fact that the evening was about to begin. Julian and Emmeline went to take their places for dinner, leaving him to wait by himself for the moment when he would make his surprise entrance, receive his award, and be interviewed for fifteen minutes. That was something he'd agreed to only on the condition that he'd be interviewed by Julian. Even so, the prospect brought him to the edge of panic. He forced himself to breathe slowly and deeply as he read through the questions they'd agreed on for the last time. What was his background? Had he always wanted to be a writer? Where had the inspiration come from for the character of Monty Silver? What were his hopes and intentions for the future? Had his success surprised him? Who were his literary heroes? All standard stuff apart from the opening question which would deal with his stammer and why they'd decided to conceal his true identity for so long.

He was aware of the sounds from the ballroom changing as the tables were cleared, glasses were filled, and the guests prepared themselves for the award ceremony. He paced around the room, before taking the opportunity to use the loo and check his appearance in the full-length mirror. Black-tie events weren't really his thing, and he never felt quite right in a tuxedo. He resisted the temptation to tinker with his bow tie one more time and contented himself with flicking his hand down his sleeve to remove a speck of dust. 'You look fine,' he told himself. 'Now just sit down and wait patiently.'

There was a double tap on the door, the prearranged signal from Emmeline to let him know that Julian was on the stage and that he needed to be ready when called. He turned the handle as quietly as he could and left the door slightly ajar. Julian had just begun speaking.

'Ladies and gentlemen, members of the Companions of Sherlock Society, distinguished guests: it is my privilege and honour this evening to introduce to you the man who is to be the recipient of the Crime Writer of the Decade award. You and his many readers already know him through his books as Matt Gee, the writer of the *Monty Silver Mysteries*. But, like so many others, you've been aware for a very long time now that Matt Gee is a pseudonym. And, like so many others, you're probably wondering who the real man is and what he's like. As his publisher, I've been privileged to get to know him very well over the last fourteen years, not just as a consummate writer of detective fiction and a master craftsman with words, but also as a good friend and someone for whom I have formed a deep respect and a genuine affection. Let me introduce to you, not Matt Gee,' he paused for dramatic effect, 'but MR MATTHEW GOLD.'

Matthew pushed open the door and walked onto the stage. Apart from the creak of the steps under his feet, there wasn't a sound in the room. He looked out at the audience to see every eye looking back at him. He guessed that many of them would have expected to see someone they already knew, an existing member of the crime-writing fraternity plying his trade under an assumed name. But no one recognised him. He thought the silence would never break and he felt an urge to turn on his heel and run. Then a woman at a table near the stage began to clap. Gradually others joined her until the entire room was giving an enthusiastic ovation. Julian came across the stage and led him by the arm to a semicircular sofa to conduct the interview. When they were both seated, he leaned into the mic and said to the amusement of the audience, 'Well, I think that'll probably be the last time Matthew Gold will stand on a stage like this and not be recognised.'

Julian waited for the laughter that greeted his comment to subside and Matthew took deep, slow breaths and prepared himself for what he knew would be the opening question.

'Matthew, everyone in this room is savvy enough to know that giving you a nom de plume was in large part related to our marketing strategy. But there was another reason, perhaps a more important reason for our decision. Do you want to speak about that?'

'Yyyes, I d-d-do…'

A ripple of nervous and embarrassed laughter ran through the ballroom. More than one person commented that if this was an attempt at a joke or an extension of that marketing strategy it was insensitive and in very bad taste. Matthew sensed their reaction and held up his hand.

'N-n-no, it's t-t-true. All mmmy life I've sssuffered from a severe st-st-stammer. And J-J-Julian wwwanted to p-p-protect me from the p-p-pressure of interviews l-l-like this. As yyyou c-c-can hear, it's d-d-difficult for mmme, especially when I g-g-get nervous – as I obv-obviously am now.'

The silence that had greeted him when he walked onto the stage was as nothing compared to the stillness that now fell on the room. The audience was looking at him and listening to him. It was the kind of attentiveness that hikers display when a sudden mist descends on the hills and every step demands their total concentration. The fifteen minutes allocated to the interview stretched into almost half an hour as he slowly and painstakingly responded to each question. His final answer when Julian asked him to sum up how he saw himself as a writer and as a human being was brief and to the point.

'W-w-words have b-b-been my p-p-problem and mmmy p-p-passion. And writing has been mmmy wwway of resolving that c-c-conflict.'

The president of the Companions of Sherlock Society joined them on the stage and invited Matthew to stand. There was, he said, nothing that he could meaningfully add to the words they'd just heard other than to read the citation for the award he was about to present:

This Crime Writer of the Decade award is presented to Matthew Gold, aka Matt Gee, for his outstanding contribution over a period of more than ten years to detective fiction through the *Monty Silver Mysteries*.

As he placed the crystal vase carefully in Matthew's hands, everyone in the room rose spontaneously to their feet. And this time their applause was immediate and sustained. Only when it subsided was it time for their unique take on proposing a toast, a ritual driven by their shared passion for the genre in which they wrote and fuelled by the copious amounts of alcohol many of them had already consumed. It was the unique seal of approval they bestowed on every recipient of one of their awards. Having first invited them to raise their glasses in their left hands, the president cleared his throat and asked in a voice that would have done justice to a regimental sergeant major: 'Whodunnit?' To which the entire company responded enthusiastically by pointing to Matthew with their right hands and calling out in unison, 'Youdunnit!' before drinking to his good health, stamping their feet loudly and banging their fists on the tables. It was, as Emmeline later remarked, an experience you would neither be able to forget nor want to repeat.

Bizarre as the climax to the evening had been, to Matthew it felt like a rite of passage, a ceremony, however unconventional, that marked his coming of age as a writer, freeing him to assume his true identity as *Matthew Gold, novelist*, and bestowing on him the status and confidence to accept the plaudits of his writing peers and the reading public. He was a middle-aged man, forty-nine years old, and at last he felt that he'd actually achieved his goal. He was a writer, a storyteller, a mystery-solver. And the reaction of the audience to the interview – to his stammering answers – had been neither derision nor sympathy. *It had been respect.* The men and women in that ballroom were writers, every one of them. And they had recognised him as one of their own, a fully fledged member of the fraternity of wordsmiths and storytellers whose achievements were all the more impressive because the most natural way to use words, normal everyday conversation, was painfully difficult for him.

It took more than an hour after the event had officially ended to receive the congratulations and shake the hand of everyone who wanted to greet him personally. When the last well-wisher had gone, he went back into the anteroom from which he'd emerged a couple of hours earlier to collect his things before retiring to the suite in the hotel he'd booked for the night. Julian and Emmeline were waiting for him.

'What a great do,' Julian said, pulling him into a hug. 'Couldn't have happened to a more deserving guy. I know you must be weary, but if you can sit down for just a minute, Emm's got something she wants to tell you before we head off.'

Matthew summoned up his last reserves of energy. It had been a long and emotionally draining evening and he wondered what she needed to say that couldn't wait until tomorrow. She was smiling, so he guessed it wasn't anything to be worried about.

'Before I let you into my secret,' she said, her smile broadening, 'I have to ask if you're busy next Saturday?'

He couldn't think why she needed to know that, but after a moment's thought he agreed that there was nothing he'd arranged to do that couldn't be altered.

'Good, 'cos I want to invite you to my wedding…' She paused long enough to let the words sink in, before adding, '… in Paris.'

Julian laughed at the look of surprise on Matthew's face who, despite his friendship with the BWs, had no idea that she was even in a serious relationship with anyone.

'You'd better explain, Emm,' he prompted, 'before poor old Matthew dies of shock. He's already had more than enough excitement for one night.'

Her explanation was simple. She and Toby had met only a couple of months ago and he'd swept her off her feet. She knew the dangers of dashing into marriage after such a whirlwind romance, but they were both in their thirties and sure of what they were doing. Toby was a doctor and about to leave for a six-month stint at a hospital in Africa and they wanted to get married before he went off. The wedding wasn't going to be an elaborate affair. Just twenty guests, close friends and family.

'And we'd love you to be there,' she concluded. 'Your relationship with Crimezone Mysteries has been the biggest single factor in making it such a success. And more important, you've become such a friend to Julian and myself. You know that Dad died last year. So Julian's going to give me away and he'll need a bit of moral support from his friends. Will you come… please?'

Matthew was finding it difficult to respond. But it wasn't his stammer. This had been one of the most memorable and happy days of his life. And now, at the end of it, to be asked to be a guest at Emmeline's wedding, to be included with their family and closest friends... There was only one response he could make.

'Of c-c-course I'll come. Thank you.'

The matter was settled and Emmeline was delighted. She and Julian would be flying to France in the middle of the week on a friend's private plane to give them time to finalise the arrangements for such a hastily organised event. And they'd book seats for their guests on a scheduled flight to Paris on Friday afternoon to make sure that everyone got there in good time for Saturday's celebrations.

Tired though he was, it took Matthew a long time to get to sleep that night. It was a day he didn't want to come to an end. And he was having difficulty in recognising and understanding how he was feeling. Simple unadulterated happiness was not an emotion with which he was familiar and it took a bit of getting used to.

chapter 21

1996

On the Thursday after being honoured by the Companions of Sherlock Society, Matthew Gold was enjoying afternoon tea in his favourite tearoom near Manchester's Piccadilly station. He had a couple of hours to while away until catching the early evening train to London where he would spend the night before meeting up with the other guests and boarding the plane that would take them to Paris for Emmeline Barrington-Williams' wedding. An assortment of newspapers from the past few days that he hadn't yet had time to read were spread out on the table in front of him. He scanned each of them in turn as he drank his Earl Grey tea and ate his delicately cut cucumber sandwiches. They made interesting and encouraging reading. The presentation of the Crime Writer of the Decade award would in itself have been sufficiently newsworthy to have merited a brief mention, particularly in the quality papers, but it would never of itself have aroused the level of interest that was evident from the column inches that had been devoted to it. The increased attention was, of course, down to the fact that the true identity of Matt Gee had been revealed.

The tabloids went for the easy headlines and the obvious puns. MAN OF MYSTERY IS MAN OF THE MOMENT and EVERYTHING HE WRITES TURNS TO GOLD were typical of their approach. The literary critic of the first of the broadsheets he picked up, however, took a more considered line:

It would be easy for the cynics to dismiss the appearance of Matthew Gold at the Companions of Sherlock Society Annual Awards Dinner as just the latest advertising gimmick from Crimezone Mysteries. Admittedly, there may well be more than a grain of truth in that assessment. Undeniably, their clever marketing strategy has played a large part in taking the Monty Silver series to the top of the bestsellers' list for much of the last decade and giving rise to the equally popular and lucrative television spin-off. Matt Gee, or Matthew Gold as we should now call him, has made a lot of money for this relatively young publishing company.

But anyone who was present in the Petram Hotel on Saturday evening was privileged to observe something much more significant and, indeed, much more moving than another publicity stunt dreamed up by one of the growing army of ad men who, in the opinion of the present writer, already have too much of an influence in the publishing world. Julian Barrington-Williams' interview with his most successful author was an illuminating insight into the mind and into the creative processes of an unusual and gifted author.

Crime fiction will never be my preferred reading and I have sometimes asked myself what is it about the *Monty Silver Mysteries* that draws me in and sets them apart from much of that genre. I still can't fully answer that question. But after Saturday evening I suspect that I'm a little closer to the answer. Matthew Gold, for whom, to use his own expression, 'words have been my problem and my passion', has found a way, against all the odds, to turn a whodunnit into an exploration of the mystery of life. The challenges he has lived with have become the alchemy that transmutes the words with which he has struggled for so long into the shining jewels that reflect the light of truth and cast a penetrating beam on the darker aspects of the human condition. His Ska-loving, mod-dressing hero is not just the late English twentieth-century progeny of Raymond Chandler's 1930s American hero. He is, in reality, nothing other than a latter-day incarnation of the seer of folk tales and fairy stories whose wisdom leads us into profound insights that would otherwise be hidden to lesser mortals like us.

It was time to pick up his suitcase and head to the station. He gave the waitress a generous tip and asked her to dispose of the newspapers, but only after carefully tearing out the article he'd just been reading and putting it in his coat pocket. That was worth keeping. It was gratifying to have his work taken seriously, though the irony was not lost on him. Those were fine words. But did his novels really deserve such approbation? Once he would have dismissed such a high-blown analysis out of hand. When he was nineteen he'd stormed out of an English literature exam at Glasgow university, staged his one-man protest against the kind of academic literary criticism that dissected books and plays and left them – he could still remember the phrase he'd coined – 'like some kind of dead animal in a laboratory'. And here he was thirty years later smiling with unfeigned pleasure at a review that his younger self would have dismissed as pretentious tosh. Had he lost the idealism of youth? Traded it for the approval of the very people he'd once held in such contempt? Bartered it for fame and an income he couldn't have dreamed of back then? Or had he just grown older and wiser, more mature and tolerant? Better not to think about that too long. He'd settle for just feeling grateful that his life was so much better than it had been in the past and that he'd achieved a level of wealth and success that could offer him some protection against the worst that the world could throw at him.

It was no more than a five-minute walk to the station and he'd timed things perfectly. The train was ready for boarding when he got there, so there would be no need to hang around on a draughty platform. He was just about to show his ticket and step through the barrier when something caught his eye. At first it didn't really register with him. It was just one of those billboards that are used to display the day's headlines and entice weary travellers to buy yet another newspaper to fill in the time on an otherwise tedious journey. He normally ignored them and hurried on by. But there was something about this particular headline that was different. For some reason he couldn't help thinking that it had something to do with him, even though he couldn't make the words compute in his mind.

He turned away from the platform and walked back to look at the billboard more closely. For the rest of his life he wished he hadn't done that. He knew it was a ridiculous notion. But he couldn't get it out of his mind. Maybe, if he'd just kept walking along the platform and boarded the 6.15 train to Euston, the words on that billboard would have faded away, leaving only a blank white poster. Maybe time would have reversed and the terrible reality that the headline was announcing to impatient commuters hurrying home from work would never have happened. *But he had gone back and time hadn't reversed.* The words were there – unalterable in bold, black capitals, and he could never forget them: MANCHESTER BROTHER AND SISTER IN MISSING PLANE OVER CHANNEL.

Even when he read the words aloud, he reasoned that statistically there had to be countless possibilities other than the one he feared. There were thousands of families in Manchester with who knew how many pairs of brothers and sisters. And there must be scores of planes flying back and forward between England and France every day. It had to be a coincidence – the kind of thing he tried to resist shoehorning into the plot of one of his novels to give the story an extra twist. He'd prove it to himself. He'd buy a newspaper and see what it said. That would put his mind at rest.

He sat on a bench with the newspaper on his lap and dared himself to read the report under the headline. It made him feel sick.

> A spokesman confirmed this afternoon that Julian and Emmeline Barrington-Williams, joint owners of the successful Manchester-based publishing company Crimezone Mysteries, were on board the six-seater light aircraft that went missing over the English Channel this morning. The pilot, Andrew Albertson, is also missing. It is not known if there were any other passengers on the plane. It is believed that the brother and sister were flying to Paris where Emmeline is due to be married to Dr Toby Camberwell on Saturday. A brief statement on the company's website said, 'While we are obviously deeply concerned, we continue to hope and pray for the best.'

There were several more paragraphs, which Matthew couldn't bear to read, focusing on the remarkable growth of Crimezone Mysteries and the recent award to their best-known author. He turned and walked towards the exit, pausing only to screw up the newspaper and throw it into the nearest bin. There was no point in travelling to London. Whoever had put together the statement for the website might be hoping and praying for the best. Life had taught him too many hard lessons for him to succumb to such wishful thinking. And he was angry with himself for being stupid enough to imagine, as he'd done on Saturday night, that real and lasting happiness was within his grasp. He'd had to face the truth about himself and about life before. Whenever he got close to anyone it always ended in tears. The most you could hope for was to survive and try to protect yourself as best you could from having your life torn apart and your heart broken over and over again.

By ten o'clock that evening the television news was reporting that parts of the wreckage of the plane had been spotted and that it was clear there were no survivors. A friend of Julian and Emmeline's who had also been invited to the wedding called to tell him what he already knew – they would not be flying to Paris on Friday and there would be no wedding the following day. He sat by himself all night feeling nothing but a deadening numbness that made any thought of sleep impossible. It was only when dawn began to break that he went into the hallway and picked up his coat from where he'd dropped it on the floor when he'd arrived home. He fumbled in the pocket and found the newspaper article he'd torn out so carefully. He walked through to the kitchen and ripped it into tiny pieces, letting them fall into the bin. And he cried as he remembered the moment in the Bute Hall three decades earlier when he'd done exactly the same thing with an exam paper full of equally worthless words. He cried for the loss of his friends. He cried for the loneliness he felt. And he cried most of all for the hideous absurdity that he could no longer ignore. He loved words – words he could forge into stories that made sense, words he could form into questions that found answers. But in the end his words, all words for that matter, amounted to nothing more than a lie, an elaborate denial of the inescapable truth. *There was no sense to the story, and there were no answers to the questions. His words were worthless and he would write no more.*

footloose

1997-2017

views from a treacherous path

chapter 22
1997

The man standing on the doorstep clutching a bunch of roses could see from the reaction of the elderly white-haired woman who answered the door that she didn't recognise him.

'Good afternoon. Can I help you?' she asked politely but uncertainly.

The caller took a moment to respond as he struggled to form his words, and the woman's eyes widened in shocked recognition.

'Goodness me,' she exclaimed, shaking her head in disbelief, 'it's Matthew Gold! We haven't seen you since Martha Smith's funeral. That's got to be... what, over fifteen years? We saw your photograph in the newspaper not that long ago, of course. But you look different, a little older...'

She stopped herself, embarrassed at her failure to hide her surprise.

'I'm sorry. I'm wittering on and forgetting my manners. It's just such a surprise to see you. Come on in. Let me take those flowers and put them in water and then I'll put the kettle on.'

Matthew apologised for calling without any prior warning and settled himself in an armchair by the window overlooking the loch while the lady of the house busied herself in the kitchen. Presumably her husband was taking advantage of the spring sunshine. He must be out walking and enjoying the Highland air. That, after all, was why they'd moved to this idyllic spot shortly after he'd retired. Forty years of teaching and being ruled by a school timetable was long enough for any man.

Agnes McFadyen came into the sitting room carrying a tray with a teapot, two cups and a plate of home-made shortbread.

'Now, I'm guessing that it's Michael you've really come all this way to see,' she said, setting the tray down on the coffee table in front of him. 'He so enjoyed reading your books and hearing of your success. And, of course, he's always appreciated your card each Christmas.'

It occurred to Matthew that at the age of fifty he still didn't know his old English teacher's first name. He'd always thought of him and always addressed him as 'Mr McFadyen'. There was something solid and reliable about that. *Mr McFadyen* – an unchanging figure in a constantly shifting world. He couldn't explain why, but just thinking of him as 'Michael McFadyen' seemed to diminish him. He was, after all, just a man. A good and decent man, certainly, but just a man. And as vulnerable as everyone else.

'Wwwell, yyyes. B-b-but it's g-g-good to sssee you too. I'm g-g-guessing he's out w-w-walking right now.'

The change in her expression signalled unmistakably that what she was about to tell him wasn't good news. She poured the tea and sat down in the armchair opposite him.

'Michael's not actually here,' she said quietly. 'He had a stroke five years ago. Got over that quite well, really. The bigger problem is that for the past couple of years he's been showing increasing signs of vascular dementia. At first it was just forgetting stuff. The kind of thing you just dismiss as what happens to everyone as they get older. But then he started having difficulty carrying out simple everyday tasks. He'd go to do something and a minute later he'd have no idea what he was supposed to be doing. About six months ago it reached the point where I couldn't cope with him at home. Two or three times he went wandering off in the night. Being as near to the loch as we are, that was a real worry. He'd made me promise that I'd put him into care if it got too much for me. I hated doing it, but it's for the best. He's been in a very nice care home since then. It's only four miles away and I drive over to visit him every day. He doesn't always know who I am. But it makes me feel better, even if five minutes after I leave he can't remember I was there.'

Matthew couldn't detect a note of self-pity or anger in her voice. There was just a dignified acceptance of the situation and a hint of regret at what had been lost. How could she be so stoic in the face of such a bitter blow? His own sadness at the news was tinged with bitter disappointment that he'd never be able to have the conversation with Mr McFadyen he'd been hoping for. Ever since the deaths of Julian and Emmeline Barrington-Williams more than a year ago, he'd been bereft of purpose, with no sense of direction and barely enough energy to get himself out of bed in the morning. The few acquaintances with whom he'd had any contact had advised him to make an appointment with his doctor. His GP had been sympathetic and had prescribed antidepressants that helped him get through each day without in any way touching the core of his despair. Coming so soon after his appearance at the Companions of Sherlock Society he'd been inundated with requests for interviews. BBC television even wanted to do a feature on him on their flagship arts programme. But he'd rebuffed every approach from the media and withdrawn more and more into himself. There had been weeks at a time when he'd never left his house. Visiting Mr McFadyen in the hope that his old mentor might say something that would help him had been a last desperate resort. Just getting his car out of the garage and setting out on a 300-mile drive had been a major effort that had all but drained his depleted reserves of energy. And now it had all been in vain. He wanted to say how sorry he was at the news and leave immediately. But before he could speak, Agnes McFadyen stood up.

'Matthew, you've come a long way and I can see how disappointed you are. Why don't you come with me to the care home? You never know, he might just recognise you. He does have fleeting moments of lucidity. He's always been proud of what you've done. It might do you both good.'

They got into Agnes' immaculately clean Mini. She handled the car confidently and he guessed that driving was a statement of her independence. She was not the kind of woman who would sit and cry and allow things to fall apart around her. Half an hour later they were pulling into the car park in front of a picturesque red sandstone single-storey building. It was set in a stunningly beautiful landscaped garden with perfectly manicured lawns that ran down to a sandy beach at the edge of the loch. When she turned off the ignition the only sounds to be heard were the lapping of the water on the shore and the birds singing in the trees. Matthew couldn't imagine a more beautiful or peaceful place in which to live out your last days. They got out of the car and he instinctively began to walk towards the entrance to the building. Agnes McFadyen slipped her arm through his, turned him around, and led him across the lawn to an area shaded by trees.

'He won't be inside on a day like today.' She shook her head and smiled. 'He'll be sat under these trees. At first the staff were worried about him wandering off like he did at home. But he never strays from this spot. It's as if beneath all the confusion he knows this place is now home for him for the rest of his days.'

Mr McFadyen was exactly where his wife had said he would be, sitting very still by himself on a wickerwork chair, his hands clasped on top of a blanket draped over his knees, looking out across the loch. His hair and beard were neatly trimmed. Clearly, he was being well cared for. It was a sight that made Matthew want to cry. He wanted to see his old English teacher looking just as he'd looked when he breezed into the classroom that first day at Bellmill Academy – his hair and beard wild and unruly, his academic gown swishing behind him. It made his heart ache to think that the old man with his legs now tucked under a blanket for warmth was once the young man who'd cocked a snook at conventional adult respectability by sitting on a table and dangling his legs in front of a class of two dozen unruly twelve-year-olds. He wanted him to stand up and call out to everyone within earshot that even a boy with a stammer deserved to be respected and listened to.

The expression on his face was peaceful but puzzled, as if he was looking for something but couldn't quite remember what it was. His wife leaned over and kissed him. He smiled gratefully but without offering any greeting or giving any indication that he knew who this kind lady was. Matthew sat down on a well-worn tree stump that had obviously served many a visitor as a rustic bench and Agnes McFadyen knelt on the grass in front of her husband, gently stroking his hand.

'Michael, I've brought Matthew Gold with me. He's travelled all the way from Manchester just to see you. You remember him, don't you?'

Matthew thought he saw a flicker of recognition, but it passed so quickly that he couldn't be sure. He wanted to say something significant to him, something that would let him know how grateful he was. More than that, he wanted to say something that might solicit some nugget of truth that he could carry away with him when he drove south again. All he managed to say was, 'Mmmr Mc-McFadyen, I th-think you're one of the wwwisest, k-k-kindest m-m-men I've ever mmmet. Thank you.'

Whether it signified recognition or not, he couldn't tell. But the old man definitely did smile in response to his words. It was a smile that took a long time to form, remained for only a second or two, and faded away without leaving a trace. His face assumed the same calm yet perplexed expression Matthew had noticed when they'd arrived a few minutes earlier. A tear began to trickle slowly down Mr McFadyen's face and, to the surprise of his visitors, he spoke. Just two words.

'Matthew…' He whispered the name and paused before adding with an almost imperceptible shake of his head, '…mystery.'

They sat with him for half an hour. Matthew and Agnes McFadyen occasionally broke the silence with the kind of inconsequential small talk that people make when visiting someone in a care home or a hospital. But the man in the wicker chair neither reacted to anything they said nor spoke again himself. A cool breeze began to blow in across the loch causing him to shiver slightly. They said their goodbyes and watched him go as a care assistant helped him gently into a wheelchair and took him back indoors.

When they got back to the house, Agnes McFadyen tried to persuade Matthew to stay for the night or at least allow her to make him a meal before he set off. It was, she said, the least she could do when he'd travelled all that way to see her husband. He declined her invitation, telling her that he had to be back in Manchester the next day for an appointment. That was untrue, but he'd found the visit emotionally costly and he wanted to be alone. They walked across the driveway together to where he'd parked his car.

'I'm so grateful to you for coming,' she said, once again slipping her arm through his. 'You know he thought the world of you. He always said you were the best student he ever had and he was so disappointed when you dropped out of university. But your success as an author more than made up for that. Since we learned that you were Matt Gee, he's made a point of reading every one of your books. He says very little these days. In fact, *Matthew* and *mystery* are the first words I've heard him say for a long time. He obviously wanted you to know he's read your novels.'

As he got into his car, he nodded his agreement with her comments and thanked her for the welcome she'd given him. Her unquestioning loyalty to her husband and her resolute determination not to succumb to despair filled him with admiration. The opinions of a woman of such character deserved his respect. But the further he drove along the road, the more he knew in his heart that Mr McFadyen's words could be construed quite differently. It was the tired shake of his head as he'd spoken the words that forced Matthew to consider other and darker interpretations. *Matthew... mystery...* Was it just the weary acceptance of a man who'd resigned himself to the long and lonely wait for death to free him from the physical and mental dungeon in which he was now locked? Was it his melancholy verdict on any attempt to make some sense out of existence? Or was he saying that Matthew himself, the boy for whom he'd done so much and from whom he'd received so little in return, was the mystery? Whatever the speaker had meant by his words, he'd certainly been right about one thing: Matthew Gold and mystery seemed to be inextricably and forever bound together.

chapter 23
1997

The driver sitting in the car parked in front of Liberty Court, a mile from Bellmill town centre, had been hoping not to attract too much attention. Having once lived there, albeit more than thirty years before, he should have known better. The sight of his immaculately maintained bright red convertible Merlin TF two-seater sports car with the roof fully retracted contrasted sharply with the far less glamorous family saloons and hatchbacks dotted along the street and served as a magnet for half a dozen schoolboys who crowded round, eager to examine the vehicle. The oldest of the boys acted as spokesman for the group.

'I like your car, mister. What is it?'

The last thing that Matthew Gold would have wanted at any time was a conversation with a bunch of lads who might be merciless in mimicking a middle-aged man with a stammer. Today the prospect of such an exchange was even less attractive. He'd left the McFadyens' house around six o'clock on the Friday evening, driven as far south as Glasgow, and decided to put up for the night in a motel on the outskirts of the city. And he'd set off that morning fully intending to be back in Manchester by Saturday afternoon. Passing the motorway sign for Bellmill, however, he turned onto the exit and decided on an impulse to make a flying visit to his home town. The house in which he'd been born was no longer standing and it seemed obvious to him, for reasons he couldn't actually have explained to anyone else, that the next best thing was to take a look at the flat where he'd lived after leaving the miners' rows. Maybe just being in the vicinity would shed some light on what, if anything, Mr McFadyen's cryptic observation the previous day might mean. A discussion about sports cars with a gang of lads from a Lanarkshire council estate was definitely not conducive to the period of quiet reflection he'd hoped for. But short of driving away at speed and risking injuring the boy who was kneeling on the ground in front of the car to get a better perspective on the contour of the bonnet, there was nothing for it but to answer the question.

'It's a M-m-merlin T-T-TF,' he said grudgingly. 'There's nnnot a l-l-lot of them around.'

He waited for the sniggers that were sure to come and got ready to tell them to move out of the way so he could drive off. But there was no sniggering, no mimicking, no derision. Either they didn't notice his stammer or they didn't care. They were just fascinated by the car and thrilled to meet someone who had the money and the good fortune to own what looked to them such an upmarket vehicle. They plied him with questions to which he responded as best he could, even resorting to making some of it up when he didn't know the real answer. When they'd found out all they wanted to know about the car, the ringleader changed tack and embarked on another line of interrogation.

'You must be rich, mister, with a car like this. Are you famous?'

The question took him by surprise. He smiled at the boy's naïve curiosity.

'Hmm… mmmaybe just a little b-b-bit famous, but nnnnot really.'

'So what are you doin' here? Famous people don't usually come here. D'you know somebody who lives here?'

'No, I d-d-don't. But a long time ago I used t-t-to lllive at 29C.'

As soon as the words had left his mouth he knew he'd made a mistake in sharing that information. He should have remembered that there was a collective memory in working-class communities like this. A shared recollection of significant or unusual events that was passed down from one generation to another and reached back many years. The group of inquisitive, chattering kids had gone quiet and they were staring at him intently. The oldest boy glanced at the others before he voiced what they were all thinking.

'Wow! You lived *there*? My dad says that he wouldn't live in that flat if you paid him. Everybody says it's haunted. The family who live there now came from some foreign place and the council moved them in and never told them what had happened there. Did you live there when it happened? When the crazy old woman killed herself?'

The blunt manner in which the question was phrased brought back the memory of the night he'd found his grandmother's body, a memory he'd long tried to suppress. It was time to leave. He turned the key in the ignition.

'I need to g-g-go,' he said, putting his foot on the accelerator and gently revving up the engine. The boys took the warning and stood aside, allowing him to drive off without injuring any of them. As he turned onto the road that led into the town he could still hear one of them calling out, 'You did! Didn't you?' And he could imagine them excitedly telling their parents that they'd met the man who'd lived at 29C Liberty Court 'when it happened' – a man who drove a red sports car and was very rich and quite famous. And neither they nor their parents would have any idea how the events of that distant night in November 1963 continued to haunt his thoughts and disturb his dreams.

The town was busy with Saturday morning shoppers as he drove along the main street and headed towards his old school. Since he was in the town, it made sense to take a look at the place, and he could be reasonably certain that he wouldn't be accosted by another bunch of nosy kids. Schools were closed at weekends. That at least hadn't changed since his day. When he pulled up in front of the building and got out of the car, however, he realised he was only half-right. Bellmill Academy wasn't just closed. *It was closed down.* Through the eight-foot-high wire mesh fence that surrounded the entire perimeter he could see heaps of litter that had been blown in by the wind and piles of debris where demolition work had already begun. He was about to get back into his car and drive off when he noticed a gap at the bottom of the fence. Someone had snipped it with wire cutters and peeled it back to leave just enough space to get through. There didn't appear to be anyone around. Reasoning that he'd never get another chance to see inside his old school, he got on his hands and knees and crawled under the hole in the fence.

No sooner had he emerged on the other side and got to his feet when he saw someone coming towards him – a caretaker or a watchman, no doubt. This, he thought ruefully, is about to be the second conversation of the morning that won't end well. He needn't have worried. The man was a former pupil of the school who'd been a few years ahead of him. Having been on his own since seven o'clock in the morning, he was happy to have someone to speak to and he fully understood the intruder's desire to take a trip down memory lane.

'I'll unlock the old Higher Grade building,' he said obligingly, reaching for the ring of keys hanging from his belt. 'They haven't started demolition on that part yet and you can take a wander through. Just be careful not to trip over anything. The electricity's turned off and some of the corridors are very dark, so you'd better borrow my torch. Bring it back when you've seen enough. I'll be over in my hut having a brew.'

Matthew made his way slowly through the hall to the classroom where he'd gone on his first day with the other twenty-three members of class 1B. The door creaked eerily as he pushed it open and the floorboards groaned with every step he took. Tiny particles of dust swirled in the sunlight streaming through the tall windows. He walked slowly across the room until he was standing in front of what remained of the blackboard. It was a bittersweet moment. He was in the same room, standing on exactly the same spot where he'd sat on the table next to Mr McFadyen, dangling his legs and telling his new classmates about his love for detective fiction. But it wasn't a classroom any longer. It was in its own way just like the man whose larger-than-life personality had filled it on that day when he'd burst through the door and introduced himself to 1B. Both were now nothing more than hollow shells from which the light had been turned off and the life had long since departed. And both had been forgotten. He couldn't imagine that anyone else from class 1B had ever bothered to visit their old English teacher or to come and look at this place. People and places would all be consigned to the same fate. Their brief existence would pass into oblivion, they would fade from memory, and every trace of their existence would be swept away by the relentless passage of time. Maybe that was what Mr McFadyen was trying to warn him about. *Matthew… mystery…* 'Matthew Gold,' he was saying, 'you're part of the mystery, you're no different from everyone and everything else. You, too, will one day be consumed by the same unstoppable process of decay.'

He didn't like what he was thinking and he hurried out of the building and back into the sunshine as quickly as he could. When he returned the borrowed torch, the watchman gave him a knowing smile.

'It's a bit spooky in there now. It feels so different to when we were kids. To be honest, I don't even like being in there myself when I do my rounds.'

Matthew nodded in agreement, gave him a £5 note for his trouble, and crawled back through the gap in the fence. He dusted himself down and got back into his car. It was turning out to be a day of confusing emotions. But he had one more visit to make before he set off home. One that would take him further back in time than either 29C Liberty Court or Bellmill Academy. It was on his way out of town, anyway. If, as he half-suspected, it no longer existed, it wouldn't add more than a minute or two to his journey.

To his surprise, Verricchia's Ice Cream Parlour looked exactly the same from the outside as he remembered it from his childhood. The unmistakable ornate doors with the name etched into the glass in elaborate lettering were unchanged. The original picture window, which allowed passers-by to glimpse the interior and enticed them to enter and savour the delights that awaited, was still intact. Matthew required no further bidding. He could do with something to lift his spirits. An ice cream sundae would cheer him up. As he walked through the door, he feared that the spell would be broken. He was sure that the booths, with their dark-wood benches covered with plush red velvet cushions and the wonderfully evocative marble-topped tables, would have been replaced by furnishings that were more hygienic and more in keeping with the last decade of the twentieth century. But nothing had been altered. Even the old gramophone was still sitting in the corner of the room, though the music was actually coming from a much more up-to-date sound system with half a dozen speakers distributed throughout the room.

There was even something familiar about the olive-skinned features of the man standing behind the counter who greeted him as he entered. Common sense told him that he couldn't be the Mr Verricchia of his childhood, who would be getting on for a hundred by now.

'Good afternoon,' the man said. He spoke with the accent and intonation patterns of the west of Scotland. Despite his resemblance to the man Matthew remembered from childhood, there was no trace of the Italian vowel sounds that had so captivated him back then. 'Take a seat and tell me what I can get you.'

As he spoke he stepped to the side, revealing a framed painting on the wall behind him. It was a portrait of the original proprietor.

'Mmmr Verricchia,' Matthew exclaimed involuntarily, pointing at the picture.

'Yes, that's my dad, Roberto. I'm his son, Marco.' He reached over the counter to shake hands. 'We had it done shortly before he died a few months ago. Do you remember him?'

'Yyyes. I used t-t-to c-c-come in here when I wwas a k-k-kid.'

There was a long pause and Matthew was aware that the man who was gripping his hand firmly was staring at him.

'You're Matthew Gold, aren't you? I thought I recognised you.' He let go of his hand and a smile slowly spread over his face. 'Have a seat and let me take your order. As soon as I've got it ready, I'll get Julia, my wife, to take over and serve the other customers. I want to sit down and talk to you.'

His smile became even wider when Matthew ordered a pot of tea, a ham sandwich, and an ice cream sundae to follow. Five minutes later the order was served and customer and café owner were sitting opposite each other. Matthew ate and drank while Marco Verricchia talked and smiled.

'My dad ran this place for more than sixty years. Every summer he'd close down for two weeks and go to the little village in Italy where he was born, but he was always glad to get back. Bellmill had become his home and this café had become his life. He was still coming in regularly and serving customers until the week before he died. He had a fund of stories about his regular customers. He really regarded them more as friends than customers. When I was a kid he used to drive me nuts with his stories, but as I got older, and especially when I took over the business, I paid a lot more attention to them. Now here's what I want to tell you…'

Matthew guessed that he was about to hear something to which he too should pay attention. The entry of a group of boisterous youngsters had raised the level of the background noise. He pushed his plate with the remains of his sandwich to one side for the moment and leaned forward so he wouldn't miss a word. As he did so, he caught sight of himself in the mirror that ran the length of the wall and realised that he was smiling almost as much as the man to whom he was listening.

'He had a lot of respect for the miners who came in,' Marco continued. 'He said that all that coal dust in their lungs gave them a taste for good Italian ice cream. Reckoned they were responsible for 50 per cent of his business back in the day. And whenever he got on to that subject, he would always talk about Jimmy Gold, who would come in regularly on a Saturday afternoon back in the fifties with his grandson after the football at Murray Park and who would always order the same thing – a pot of tea, a sandwich, and an ice cream sundae for his boy. My old man thought the world of Jimmy. *Salt of the earth* – that's how he used to describe him. And he had a real soft spot for Jimmy's grandson, Matthew. He would tell us that he always knew that kid would go a long way. Always knew he wouldn't let his stammer stop him. Always knew that one day he'd find a way of getting the words out. And when that happened, Dad would insist, that kid would have something worth saying.'

Matthew grinned appreciatively and Marco Verricchia paused and slid out of the booth, adding that there was something he needed to show him. He reached behind the counter and returned with two paperback books – *The Priest and the Princess* and *The Poisoning of Mary Morrison*. He laid them on the marble-topped table and picked up where he'd left off.

'Every time Dad told us about Jimmy Gold, he'd wonder what became of his grandson. When I saw all that stuff in one of the Sunday papers last year about Matt Gee really being Matthew Gold, I recognised the name and showed it to him. He was pleased as punch.' Marco put his hand on top of the books he'd laid on the table and laughed. 'Even after all that time living over here, he never really mastered reading English. He could manage newspaper headlines, not much more than that. But he went straight out and bought these books. He kept them under the counter and often when we weren't too busy, he'd take them out, sit down with a customer who'd time to kill, and tell them how the kid with the stammer who came into his shop had become a famous author. And he faithfully watched the *Monty Silver Mysteries* on TV. He'd have loved to have met you.'

After his experiences over the past twenty-four hours, Matthew was grateful for such warm-hearted, unfeigned affirmation. There was so much that he'd forgotten about his birthplace, and Marco, who'd clearly inherited his father's ability to chat with customers and put them at their ease, was a fount of knowledge about goings-on in Bellmill both past and present. The more Marco talked, the more the memories came flooding back into Matthew's mind and the more questions he asked. Verricchia's Ice Cream Parlour, Marco explained, had a unique place in the life of the town. In his father's words: 'People go to the pub to drink and argue about football; they go to church to find strength and pray to God; but they come to an Italian café to eat the best ice cream and talk to anyone who'll listen.'

Matthew had never found the noisy atmosphere of a pub a congenial environment for a man with a stammer; and, like his grampa, he'd never felt particularly at home in churches; but he was definitely enjoying the ice cream and he was talking far more about his childhood and the events of the past eighteen months than he'd intended. The time flew by and he was surprised when he realised that they'd been talking for more than an hour and the café had all but emptied of customers. He thanked Marco for the best conversation and the best ice cream sundae he'd had in years and was getting ready to leave when his genial host suddenly became more serious.

'Forgive me if I'm intruding in any way. But there's someone you might want to talk to while you're here. Bob Urquhart is well into his eighties now. He was a miner in his twenties, got made redundant when the last of the pits closed, took up his education again and trained as a teacher. Since he retired, he's become the town's unofficial historian. Comes in here quite often. Says it's the best place to pick up the local gossip and find out what's happening. When all that stuff was in the paper about you, he was really interested. He didn't say a lot, but I got the impression he knows a bit about your family history. Why don't you stay for a day while you're up this way? My dad would be chuffed to know that you've been in his café and enjoyed his ice cream. And, unlike my dad, my wife *has* read your books and loved them. She'll be delighted to have you stay in our home. And I'll give Bob a ring and arrange for you two to meet tomorrow.'

Despite his initial protestations that he couldn't possibly presume on their kindness, Matthew eventually accepted Marco's offer of hospitality. He fell asleep that night in the comfortable guest bedroom of the flat above Verricchia's Ice Cream Parlour, remembering the little boy who would arrive there on his grampa's shoulders, and wondering what more he might learn about that little boy when a new day broke.

chapter 24
1997

Bob Urquhart was the kind of man you couldn't help but notice when he lurched into a room, his gangly, uncoordinated limbs appearing to be only partially under his control.

More than six feet tall and thin as a rake, with a shock of thick black hair and a pencil moustache that accentuated his gaunt features, he reminded Matthew of a photograph of George Orwell he'd once seen in a newspaper article about *Animal Farm*. His ill-fitting tweed jacket and baggy corduroy trousers conveyed the unmistakable impression that this was a man who required nothing more from his clothes than that they covered his body, afforded him a basic protection from the elements, and had pockets sufficiently large to contain a couple of notepads and the latest book he was reading.

The Verricchias had arranged for the two men to meet in the front room of their flat, and Marco had prepared Matthew for what to expect.

'It's always best to talk to Bob somewhere private,' he suggested. 'He doesn't really have a volume control and when he gets going there's no stopping him. But he's a good man who's committed to Bellmill and to finding out its story. He was an active member of the communist party in his youth and he's still pretty far to the left on most things. You can guess that I don't see eye-to-eye with him on a lot of stuff. But he's one of the most principled and intelligent men I know, and he's highly respected by most folk in the town.'

Five minutes into their meeting, it was clear to Matthew that Marco had painted an accurate picture of Bob Urquhart. This was a man with an insatiable curiosity, a passion for justice, and a ruthless honesty that was uninhibited by what he would have regarded as bourgeois convention. After asking Matthew a few direct questions about his writing, he came straight to the point.

'Well, I've read a couple of your books. Not really to my taste. I think you could put your talent to better use. But I will admit, you do know how to write. And from what I've been able to glean about your grandparents, I think Jimmy Gold would be proud of you. Maggie Gold? I'm not so sure, but you never know.'

Matthew decided his best response would be to gratefully accept the praise and ignore the criticism, especially since Bob's last remark opened the door to what he hoped would be a conversation that would go some way to answering a question to which he wanted to know the answer.

'Thanks fffor the c-c-compliment,' he responded. 'B-b-but I'm rrreally interested in what you've learned about mmmy g-g-grandparents and my ch-ch-childhood.'

Bob Urquhart reached into his inside jacket pocket and brought out a wad of tightly rolled A4 sheets held together with a thick red elastic band.

'For a long time, to the surprise of some people who don't like my politics and don't really know me, I've been interested in the history of some of the Christian congregations in the town. Especially those that aren't part of the Church of Scotland or the other more mainstream denominations. They interest me for several reasons: they're a fascinating study in group dynamics and they've contributed a lot that's good to life in Bellmill. But they're often full of warnings of how people who are committed to a cause can end up jettisoning their highest principles and ill-treating other people in pursuit of that cause. I had to acknowledge a long time ago that communist regimes could be guilty of hideous crimes against humanity in pursuit of their aims. But I've sometimes seen the same tendency up close and personal in some of these religious groups.'

He unrolled and flattened the sheets of paper and handed them to Matthew with an apology for the coffee stains on the top sheet.

'These are some of the relevant records that I've spent a lot of time going through. You can read them for yourself when you get time, but I'm happy to give you a precis of what's in there, if that's what you'd like.'

Matthew assured him that that was exactly what he'd like, and Bob began to share the results of his research.

'In many ways, the Bellmill Holiness and Bible Fellowship, to use their official title, is fairly typical of what I've often found in these groups. They separated from the local kirk in the early 1900s because of what they saw, probably not without some justification from what I've uncovered, as the nominal and shallow Christianity of the minister at that time and many of the members. Two things made them a particularly interesting case study from my angle. The first was that they kept meticulous records of everything from their foundation until the last few members died and they folded in 1979. That's obviously a great help to someone like me. The second thing was – and this in my experience is almost unique for a group like this – that they were initially driven almost as much by a concern for the poor and for social justice as by a desire for personal moral purity. It's clear from their records that they did a lot of charitable work in their early years, helping people in some of the most deprived areas of the town. One of their members even stood for and was elected to the town council in 1910 and championed some fairly radical causes.'

Just at that moment, Julia Verricchia came in with tea and sandwiches and pastries from the café downstairs. The offer of a cup of tea was one of the few things that would stop Bob Urquhart in full flow, and a respite was agreed to give opportunity to enjoy the hospitality on offer. After ten minutes, suitably refreshed by the lunch, he was ready to pick up his story again.

'However, there was a change of leadership around 1915 and things began to go in a very different direction. It started with a decision not to permit music in their worship, other than the unaccompanied singing of psalms. Any direct engagement with the life of the local community, particularly in the area of local politics, was viewed with suspicion. The slogan that occurs again and again in their records is a verse from chapter six of Paul's Second Letter to the Church at Corinth: "Wherefore come out from among them, and be ye separate, saith the Lord, and touch not the unclean thing". I've read it so often in their documents. That's why an agnostic like me can give you chapter and verse. "Come out from among them" seems to have become something of a motto and they withdrew fairly rapidly into a rigid legalism. Their censure was directed particularly towards pastimes that other people would see as innocent pleasures: going to the cinema or a football match or a fairground, even listening to the wireless apart from news broadcasts, were all taboo. Women were forbidden to use make-up or wear any form of what was judged to be "worldly adornment" on pain of being disfellowshipped. And that's where your grandparents come into the picture...'

He paused to show Matthew some old sepia photographs of forty or so unsmiling people sitting in rows in what looked like a wooden hut, each of them holding a large black leather-bound Bible conspicuously in their right hand. The women were seated on one side of the room wearing hats and long black dresses and the men on the other side in dark suits with their jackets buttoned up. Their uniform attire and solemn expressions made it hard to tell their ages or to distinguish one person from another. He pointed first to one of the women and then to one of the men in the photograph.

'That's your grandmother and there's your grandfather. I think it would have been taken around 1920.'

'B-b-but that's impossible,' Matthew protested. 'G-G-Grampa was n-never p-p-part of the Fffellowship.'

'Well, actually he was,' Bob insisted. 'I've been able to piece the story together from the records of the Fellowship and from speaking to people whose family members were involved with them at one time or another. It's definitely not a happy-ever-after story, but I suspect it's one you need to know if you want to understand who they were and who you are.'

Bob Urquhart walked across the room and quietly closed the door that Julia had left slightly ajar when she'd brought in lunch. This was obviously a moment for privacy. He sat down, crossed his long legs, and settled himself into his chair again. Knowing that this was not a man to sugar-coat his account with easy platitudes, Matthew tried to prepare himself for whatever he was about to hear. But instead of launching into his story, Bob produced something else from his pocket. Unlike the untidy bundle of notes he'd handed him a few minutes earlier, this was a sealed envelope.

'It's all there on a couple of sheets of A4 paper. I think maybe it's better for you to read it for yourself rather than me tell it to you, so I've typed it up. That'll be better than just trying to remember what I've said. If you'd like to read it now, then I can answer any questions you might have.'

Matthew's hands were trembling slightly as he opened the envelope, unfolded two sheets of A4 paper and began to read:

Maggie Thompson was the only child of one of the families the Fellowship had helped with food and clothing. Her mother died of tuberculosis when Maggie was only ten, leaving her in the less-than-attentive care of her hard-drinking father. The Fellowship became by default her surrogate family, giving her a sense of worth and identity she would never otherwise have had. By the time she reached her mid-teens she had made a public confession of faith as required by the Fellowship and was fully immersed in the life of the congregation. There were few other young people of her age in the services and she was understandably drawn to James Gold, who was a year older and who sat dutifully beside his parents and younger sister every Sunday. She couldn't help but notice that sometimes, when the other members of the Gold family were focused on what was being said from the pulpit, he would find an opportunity to smile across at her from the other side of the room.

It was still a surprise to her when one Sunday, the day of her sixteenth birthday, he asked her if she would like to go for a walk with him. Having little experience of the opposite sex, she was both flustered and flattered by his attentions. She accepted his invitation to meet the following evening and agreed to keep their rendezvous a secret. James' intentions were entirely honourable and their conduct that evening was innocent – apart from two things. Maggie decided to let her long black hair down over her shoulders and James persuaded her that they should go to see a film in the Alhambra Picture House. Those two actions meant that they had breached the strict moral code of the Fellowship, which demanded that a woman should keep her hair neatly tied in a bun behind her head and forbade attendance at places of what they deemed to be 'worldly entertainment'. The elders of the Fellowship had long ago foreseen the temptation that would inevitably result from the touch of luxurious flowing hair on a young man, particularly in surroundings where the only light came from the flickering images of questionable conduct projected onto a cinema screen.

Of course, neither James nor Maggie intended to tell anyone of their clandestine tryst, but the member of the congregation who happened to be passing and saw them as they were entering the cinema had no such compunction about reporting what she had witnessed. They were hauled before the elders to give an account of themselves and warned that any repeat of such wanton behaviour would result in excommunication from the Fellowship. For Maggie, the thought of expulsion from the community that had given her so much and in which her entire life was bound up was more than she could bear. She agreed to the act of public repentance that was demanded of her, and the next Sunday she stood up in front of the entire congregation, openly confessed her sin and asked for forgiveness.

James, however, resisted their pressure. He had previously incurred the displeasure of the leadership, who regarded all fiction as 'worthless lies', when they learned from his parents of his liking for novels. He had ignored their counsel then and he was in no mood to listen to them on this occasion. He refused to accept that he'd done anything wrong or to accede to the demands being made of him. He stormed out of the meeting and, despite the pleas of his parents, he never *went back. His actions proved costly and strained his relationship with his family to breaking point. After a few months he left home and went to live with a relative who had no links with the Fellowship.*

But the bond between the young couple had not been completely broken. After a year or so they began to meet secretly again and when James turned eighteen they got married without the prior knowledge or consent of their parents. There were rumours that Maggie was pregnant and had miscarried but there is no proof of that being the case. Nonetheless, her marriage to a man who was not only an 'outsider' but also a 'backslider' earned the condemnation of the elders and Maggie was asked to leave. At the time, James was employed in the offices of the local steelworks and had been selected for management training. It was, however, not a well-paid job and he needed to find suitable accommodation for himself and his new wife. The only route he could take that provided a quick solution was to go into coal mining, which paid better money and meant that he qualified for one of the tied houses owned by the mining company. Early in 1923 James and Maggie Gold moved into 121 Pit Road, the house at the very end of the miners' rows. It was the house most couples wanted to leave when a less exposed and warmer house became available. But it was where they would spend the rest of their married life together.

Things seemed to go well for the first few years, but Maggie was racked with guilt over her decision to marry and her subsequent expulsion from the Fellowship. Without telling her husband, she met with the elders and pleaded to be readmitted. It was a lengthy process and they deliberated for many months before reaching a decision. In the end, she was reinstated into the congregation, but not without a strong reprimand that would hang over her for the rest of her life. She had made her bed and would have to lie in it – though the elders of the Bellmill Holiness and Bible Fellowship phrased their considered judgement in more biblical terminology. She had, they recorded in the minutes of the meeting, 'allowed herself to be unequally yoked with an unbeliever'. Divorce was not an option, they told her, and she must 'make her godly life at home a constant rebuke to her husband and so bring him to repentance'.

The salvation of James may have been the goal the elders had in mind, but Maggie's attempts to follow their direction had the opposite effect. Her efforts to be 'a rebuke' appeared to him and, indeed, to everyone else with whom she had any contact, as nothing better than self-righteous pride and an unattractive piety. Her unconcealed displeasure at his willingness to answer to Jimmy – the name his fellow colliers had bestowed on him – rather than to the more formal James merely served to confirm him in his estimation of her conduct.

If Jimmy endured his suffering with a stoic silence, their only child, Sarah, responded in an altogether different manner. Unable to live up to the impossibly exacting standards set for her, and feeling unloved and unwanted by her mother, she reacted with open rebellion. The last few years of her brief life were marked by a succession of defiant confrontations with authority *and a series of promiscuous relationships with older men. More than one neighbour commented after she died in childbirth that, sad as her untimely death was, at least it released her from the destructive influence of her overbearing mother who had made her short time on earth a misery.*

From start to finish, this has been a sorry saga of the destructive impact on three lives of what may have begun as a well-meaning attempt by sincere people to form a radical Christian congregation but which all too rapidly degenerated into a legalistic and controlling religious sect.

When he got to the end of the document, Matthew sat for a full five minutes without speaking, trying to put his confused thoughts into some kind of order. There were things he could understand for the first time: why his grandparents' marriage had been so unhappy; why his grampa had never gone to the Fellowship and never allowed him to go; why his grandmother had been so hard and unbending; why in the end it had all become too much for her. But on a deeper level it simply threw him into greater confusion and brought him face to face once again with the recurring question: why? Why do things always turn bad? Why are good and bad so tied together and messed up that sometimes you can't tell one from the other?

To those questions he could find no resolution. But there was one question that he could ask to which there might be an answer. A question he'd never asked before. A question he was nervous about asking now. But he would ask it of this man. Bob Urquhart wouldn't shirk from giving him an answer.

'Yyyou've d-d-done a lot of research. Thank you. B-b-but did yyyou ever fffind out who mmmy f-f-father was?'

'No, I didn't.' Bob shook his head and paused, as if he was wondering whether he should amplify his brief answer. When he did speak again, he spoke slowly and quietly, unlike his normal animated responses. 'I did actually try. But the fact was, there were almost limitless possibilities. Your mother was a very troubled and promiscuous young woman and there were so many men. And, from all I've been able to gather, they would often ply her with alcohol. It's unlikely that she would have known who the father was. I'm sorry, but maybe it's better not to know…'

His voice trailed off, leaving Matthew to draw his own conclusions. They sat quietly for a few moments longer before Bob stood up and suggested it was probably the right time for him to go. Matthew thanked him again and they shook hands. Just as he reached the door, Bob turned around. There was something else he wanted to say.

'When I started researching the Bellmill Holiness and Bible Fellowship, the story of your grandparents and your mother emerged as a particularly disturbing example of the damage such sects can do to people. It was only when I was down in the café one day chatting to Roberto, and he was showing me your books that he'd just bought and telling me about how you used to come in as a kid, that it dawned on me that you must be Jimmy Gold's grandson. I'd read the article about you in the paper, but I'd never tied it all together in my mind. And then, of course, Marco called me yesterday and asked if I'd come over today. I just want to say it's been a privilege to meet you and I hope that what I've been able to tell you is some kind of help to you.'

They shook hands again, even more firmly this time, and he left. Matthew smiled wryly to himself as he heard the departing visitor stomping noisily down the stairs. He was grateful to have had the conversation and to have heard the story. But whether or not it would prove to be helpful, he had no idea. He tried to work out where it left him. He existed as the result of a series of happenings that culminated in a disturbed young woman copulating with a man whose name she may not have known and whose face she probably wouldn't have been able to remember the next day. He wasn't what polite people called 'an unplanned pregnancy'. He wasn't even the result of a casual affair. He was the unwanted consequence – the inconvenient biological by-product – of an act of abuse and lust that involved neither love nor a genuine physical attraction and ultimately cost the life of Sarah Gold. And yet… *he existed*. Without the Bellmill Holiness and Bible Fellowship and its controlling leadership, without the ill-matched and unhappy marriage of James Gold and Maggie Thompson, without the sordid one-night stand of a troubled teenager and the unknown man who was happy to take advantage of her – without all that chaos and misery he would never have been born.

People knew him as the man who'd created an unforgettable character, a slick-talking private eye who could find all the answers and solve every mystery. He'd been proud of that. But it was nothing more than escapist entertainment. He had no answers in the real world where life and death and right and wrong were locked together in a macabre dance in which it was all but impossible to distinguish one from the other. And now he was facing the deepest conundrum of all – himself. If he'd been about to write his autobiography, he knew what his title would be: *The Mystery of Matthew Gold.*

chapter 25
1999

Shortly after eleven o'clock on the 11th August 1999, people all across Britain were readying themselves for an event that wouldn't happen again in their lifetime. In London, office workers left their desks and gathered on the bridges over the Thames. In Brighton, holidaymakers on the beach finished their ice creams, put on their sunglasses and looked to the heavens. In Wiltshire, 10,000 hippies and latter-day druids stood silent and expectant among the great boulders of Stonehenge and waited for the moment to arrive. And all of them watched in awe as the moon slipped between the sun and the earth and the world around them grew eerily dark and quiet. It was over in less than two and a half minutes, but it would stay in their memories for the rest of their lives.

Matthew Gold, however, missed the total solar eclipse, the like of which would not happen in the skies over Britain for another ninety years. He missed it by only a few minutes and only because he felt a little unwell. He'd intended to pause on his drive to a walking holiday in the Scottish Highlands, to pull into a lay-by on the A9 and witness the event that had been so enthusiastically anticipated by the media. But he'd been feeling below par on the journey. Nothing serious – just a slight discomfort, a touch of indigestion, an odd ache in his jaw. All the same, he didn't fancy standing beside his car by the side of the road to view the astronomical phenomenon that was about to take place. He decided to turn off the main road and head into Pitlochry, which was only a couple of miles out of his way. He'd discovered a nice café that did a decent pot of Earl Grey when he'd been in this part of Scotland last year. There'd be time for a tea break and a loo stop. He'd take two paracetamol with his tea and he'd feel better after that. He could see the eclipse as he walked back to the car.

As he'd hoped, he began to feel a little more normal when he'd taken the pills and drunk his tea. He did wonder if he might have flu coming on when he suddenly shivered and the room seemed to darken, but it passed after a couple of minutes and he put it down to his imagination. It wasn't until he stepped outside again and heard people talking about the gloom that had just passed over the town that he realised what had caused the temporary drop in temperature. The eclipse had actually happened while he was in the café. He'd miscalculated the time. *A once in a lifetime event and he'd missed it!* Oh well, from what he could overhear, it hadn't been a particularly spectacular sight in this part of the country anyway, and missing it would make no difference to the rest of his life. He was right about that. What he didn't realise at that moment was that it wasn't the only thing he'd miss that day.

He got into his bright red Merlin TF convertible and set off on his journey north again. It was more than ten years old now but he'd no intention of changing it for a later model. He loved that car. In the last year particularly, it had become his means of escape. It carried him out of his familiar surroundings to lonely and distant places. Places like the cottage on the very edge of the west coast to which he was heading now, places where he could get away from everything and everyone. More than that, it was *in itself* an escape. Driving at speed with the roof down, the audio system turned up full blast and the wind rushing past his face was not just what the magazines he'd read in his youth would have described as 'an unforgettable motoring pleasure'. It was the most effective way he knew to shut out the noises in his head, to ignore the questions that wouldn't go away, to flee from the mystery that stalked him everywhere.

As soon as he got back onto the A9, he brought his speed up to seventy. Now he was ready to go. A glance in the mirror assured him that there wasn't a police car behind to worry about. He turned on the CD player and set it to a volume that was loud enough to drown out the snarl of the engine. Then he rammed his foot on the accelerator and watched with satisfaction as the needle on the speedometer shot up to ninety-five. These were the best moments he knew in life. Moments that he wished could last forever. Moments in which everything else stood still, left behind as he sped past, oblivious to anything but the sheer exhilaration of the momentum that was carrying him forward. Today, however, something was hindering his break for freedom from the troubling thoughts that pursued him wherever he went. At first, he couldn't think what it was that was thwarting his attempts. But slowly his brain began to recognise the signals that were coming from his body. He was feeling ill, just like he'd felt earlier. But worse. Much worse. He was struggling to work out how to respond to what was happening to him. *And that must have been when he missed it – missed the sign warning drivers that the dual carriageway was about to revert to a single carriageway.* That was when he swerved a split second too late to avoid the oncoming car. He caught the side of the driver's door and sent it skidding off the road.

He quickly pulled onto the hard shoulder and got out of the car. Traffic coming in both directions had already stopped, allowing him to run across the road to check on the other vehicle, a small black family saloon that was tilted at a precarious angle on the sloping grass verge with its engine still running and its doors still closed. He hesitated, afraid of what he might discover. Someone brushed past him, opened the passenger door and reached towards the young woman driver who was badly shaken but mercifully seemed unhurt. 'My baby, my baby,' she kept repeating. To Matthew's relief the baby was still safely strapped in the child seat, crying and confused by what had just happened but, like his mother, unharmed. The fury of the elderly man who was approaching him, however, ensured that the instant release of tension he felt was short-lived.

'You passed me a mile back on the road,' he shouted, pointing his finger at him. 'You were driving at a crazy speed. You're lucky you didn't kill someone. I've called

999. The police and the ambulance are on their way. Don't you dare drive off.'

Matthew was about to assure him that he'd no intention of leaving the scene when the clamour around him began to recede into the distance and the light slowly faded into an impenetrable darkness. He remembered nothing after that until he woke up twenty-four hours later in hospital. The serene and reassuring voice of the doctor speaking to him was in stark contrast to the angry words thrown at him by the irate motorist before he'd lost consciousness.

'Mr Gold, you're in the cardiac unit at Perth Royal Infirmary. You've been in a road accident. You were uninjured, but you did have a heart attack. You got to us just in time. You'll be with us for a few weeks while we get you stabilised. But there's no reason why, with proper care and rehabilitation, you shouldn't make a full recovery.'

Six weeks later he was back at home in Manchester, and three months after that he was deemed to be sufficiently recovered to return to Scotland to answer the charge of dangerous driving. He pleaded guilty and offered his profound apologies to the young mother and her baby whose lives he had put at risk. As he stood in the dock to receive his sentence, the voice he now heard was neither angry nor serene, but earnest and solemn. The judge was clearly determined that he should not leave the court in any doubt as to the gravity of his offence or the jeopardy in which he had placed others.

'Matthew Gold, you have been convicted of a serious offence. You were driving dangerously at more than thirty miles an hour above the legal speed limit, causing great risk to yourself and inevitably to other innocent people.

Had your conduct resulted in the death of the occupants of the car with which you collided, you would undoubtedly be facing a lengthy custodial sentence. It is only by good fortune that such a tragic outcome did not result from your irresponsible actions. However, having taken into account the medical reports of your state of health at the time of the offence, which may, in part, have impaired your judgement, and the fact that you are still in recovery from the heart attack that you suffered, I have decided to err on the side of what some will consider to be undue and undeserved leniency. I am not going to send you to prison. Knowing you to be a man of some considerable means, I am imposing a fine of £30,000 and disqualifying you from driving for two years, after which you must take an extended driving test before you regain your licence. You can be sure that if you are ever found guilty of such an offence again, you will not escape a lengthy custodial sentence.'

That evening he walked from the court to be greeted by a phalanx of newspaper photographers. The next morning, he woke to a variety of sensationalist tabloid headlines, ranging from WEALTHY MYSTERY MAN WALKS FREE to CALLS FOR JUDGE TO BE REMOVED AFTER MISCARRIAGE OF JUSTICE. For the next couple of weeks he was besieged by reporters whenever he tried to leave home. And after a month, at the end of his tether and unable to bear it any longer, he left the country for an extended vacation until the heat would die down. He travelled alone, visited five continents, stayed in the best hotels, and took little pleasure in anything he saw or did. He did not return to England for almost a year.

chapter 26
2000

The young man showing the property on a sunny August morning had either practised long and hard to become fluent in the grandiose idioms beloved of his trade or he'd simply memorised his script by rote. Either way, he was obviously determined to give his client the benefit of what he'd learned. Even as they drove into the estate, he was in full flow.

'I think you will agree, Mr Gold, that this aspirational development is the very epitome of Robyn Homes' commitment to traditional building values. At the same time, each luxuriously appointed house has been designed with modern living very much in mind, and offers stunning individual elevational finishes combined with light and airy interiors that offer the perfect place to work, play and relax in style. We believe that The Rookery is set to become one of the most sought-after places to live in the UK.'

Matthew Gold listened wearily, wondering who had written this stuff and whether anyone ever took it seriously, and thinking cynically to himself that he'd rather be afflicted by his stammer than spout this kind of meaningless and pretentious garbage. He'd settled on this part of Wilmound not because of the persuasive rhetoric of the estate agent's brochure, but because he thought it promised the peace and quiet he longed for. And he'd decided to view this particular house in the newly built estate mainly because it was tucked at the end of a no through road that would afford him the maximum amount of privacy. He wasn't disappointed in the property. Its relative seclusion was exactly what he was looking for, and though he would have described it in less florid language than that used by the over-enthusiastic estate agent, he had to agree that it had been built and finished to the highest standards. The quality was, of course, reflected in the price, but that was no problem to a man who had more than enough money in the bank to keep him in comfort for the rest of his days and who had no need to negotiate a mortgage. A couple of months after viewing and buying the property, he'd sold his previous much more modest dwelling and taken possession of Number 7, The Rookery. Over the next year he spared no expense in having the garden professionally landscaped, installing a fully equipped home cinema and filling his house with bespoke furnishings and an impressive array of gadgets, only a few of which he ever actually used. Here, he hoped, he could spend the rest of his life without being disturbed by prying newspaper reporters, inquisitive neighbours or intrusive thoughts.

Apart from a few minor interruptions to the closed and sheltered life he'd planned for himself, the first two of those aspirations were more or less fulfilled. And during his waking hours he successfully managed to shut out most of the unpleasant memories and unwanted emotions that threatened the steady rhythm of his existence. It was the hours of darkness, however, that proved to be the breach in the otherwise impregnable walls he'd built around himself. No matter how much he tried to convince himself that the past was closed and the future was secure, that his writing days were over and his search for answers was ended, he could not escape the recurring dream that relentlessly lay in wait for him whenever he closed his eyes. He never went to bed before midnight and rarely dropped off to sleep before one o'clock, but all too often he would wake up with a start two or three hours later, bathed in a cold sweat and feeling his heart beating rapidly in his chest.

His nightmare always followed the same sequence of events. He was sitting in front of his old manual typewriter by an open window in the flat above the launderette where he'd lived so many years before. Beside the typewriter there was a pile of papers, the manuscript of a novel he'd just completed. A sudden gust of wind blew in through the window, scattering the pages across the room. He closed the window, got down on all fours, retrieved the papers and painstakingly put them all back in the right order again. But then there was always that terrible moment when he realised that he had hadn't found the most important sheets of paper:

> *There were always three pages missing. The last three pages. The pages that made sense of the story. The pages where all the questions were answered and the mystery was solved. The pages that tidied things up, brought*

*everything to a satisfactory conclusion. Even worse,
try as he might, he couldn't for the life of him remember
a sentence or even a single word that was on those
missing pages.*

Occasionally he'd get up, go to the loo, come back to bed
and manage to fall asleep fairly quickly. But more often
than not, he'd end up in the kitchen drinking tea and
waiting for the knot in his stomach to ease before going
back to bed and trying to get a couple of hours more rest.
There was hardly a week that went past when he didn't
have that dream. The more it happened, the harder he tried
to push it out of his mind. And the harder he tried, the
more it happened.

He toyed with the idea of seeking professional help –
some kind of therapy or hypnosis, anything that might rid
him of the problem. But that would involve him in talking
about his life with somebody, and that was the last thing
he wanted. That at least was how he rationalised his
reluctance to deal with the problem. Sometimes, when he
sat alone in the kitchen in the early hours of the morning,
he wondered if he really wanted to be free of the dream.
What if it was telling him something? Was there something
he'd lost or never had? Something just out of reach and out
of sight? Something deep in his subconscious that he
lacked the courage to face? But he quickly dismissed those
questioning thoughts as meaningless psychobabble or
merely the confusion brought on by the lack of sleep.

For the next seventeen years his life settled inexorably
into a repetitive and constricting pattern as he withdrew
ever deeper into himself and retreated ever further from
any meaningful engagement with people in the world

around him. His mother's death in childbirth, his grampa's heart attack, his grandmother's suicide, the deaths of Julian and Emmeline Barrington-Williams – he felt a responsibility for all of them, even though he tried to tell himself that made no sense. The desperate cries of the mother for her baby in the crash on the A9 haunted him. That they were alive was the result of sheer blind chance and no thanks to him. And as for his writing, Bob Urquhart was probably right – maybe he could have put his talent to better use and produced something of more worth than a series of crime mysteries that would be forgotten and unread in a few short years. His life amounted to nothing of lasting worth or significance. In his darkest moments he summed it up in one bleak sentence. He had been hurt himself and he'd inflicted hurt on others. The best he could hope for was to live out his days without being hurt again or causing any more hurt to anyone else.

He employed a housekeeper who came in for a few hours every day and a gardener who worked one or two days every week to make sure that things were kept in the good order with which he liked to surround himself. He treated them courteously but spoke little to either of them apart from what was necessary to pass on his instructions and make sure they were paid. Most mornings, if the weather permitted, he would walk a mile or two, often stopping halfway round to visit a conveniently situated tea shop. And every evening without fail he would make his way to the restaurant in the town centre where he would eat dinner alone at a table reserved for him in the corner by the window. When he was at home, he would pass the time reading or watching television programmes and films in the comfort of his sound-proofed home cinema. Sometimes he would listen to the Ska music he'd once loved so much, but his pleasure in listening diminished as the years passed. Between October and April every year he would take a couple of extended holidays to escape the cold and to find some sunshine, but he was always glad to come back home to his settled routine.

He was neither happy nor unhappy. Nothing made him laugh and nothing made him cry. He no longer loved or hated. He had lost the capacity to be delighted or disappointed. He had chosen to inhabit a state of limbo in which the normal human responses to life were held in abeyance. He was detached from people who might demand his attention and immune to anything that might touch his emotions. He was passing through the world rather than living in it. *He was safe.* But he had become a man with a mind and body but no soul.

love-struck

2017-2019

vistas from a new perspective

chapter 27

2017

Saturday 11th March 2017 was a mild, dry day in the north-west of England. One of those days that carries the promise that winter is drawing to a close and spring is just around the corner. It was also Matthew Gold's seventieth birthday, an anniversary he'd no intention of celebrating. His recurring nightmare had disturbed his rest yet again and, though he'd not slept well, he followed his long-established routine and set off on his morning walk at precisely 9.45. Half an hour later he reached The Sanctuary Tearoom that nestled by the side of Wilmound's medieval church and stepped inside. The place was empty apart from an elderly man he didn't recognise sitting by the window, who greeted him as he entered.

'Good morning,' he said in a soft, hoarse voice. 'A fine day for this time of year.'

Matthew guessed from the slight slurring of his speech and the flat monotone in which his words were delivered that the speaker was suffering from Parkinson's disease, a suspicion that was confirmed by his trembling hands when he raised his cup to his mouth. He'd no desire to exchange pleasantries with a total stranger, so he merely nodded his agreement and sat down at a table on the opposite side of the room. There were few things he could imagine that would be more tedious and tiring than a dialogue between someone with Parkinson's and a man with a severe stammer. He settled himself in his customary manner and in less than five minutes the waitress had brought a pot of Earl Grey tea and a scone to the table without needing to take his order. She knew better than to try to engage her customer in conversation. Experience had taught her that, provided he was left alone, there was usually a decent tip to be picked up from the table after he'd gone.

The Sanctuary Tearoom had become a favourite of Matthew's, not just because it was conveniently situated on his walk or even for the excellent quality of the tea it served. Set back from the main thoroughfare and overshadowed as it was by the old church, it had the benefit of being a quiet refuge in an increasingly strident world. Young mums with their squawking babies and people who needed to listen to music while they ate and drank patronised the coffee shops in the town centre, leaving The Sanctuary as a haven for those who needed neither background noise nor any other entertainment to accompany their mid-morning refreshment. But this morning, to his surprise and irritation, he could hear the sound of children's singing coming from the nearby church. Noticing that the door had been left ajar, he walked over to close it and shut out the noise, when something about the singing stopped him in his tracks. It was some kind of hymn; he could hear that now. But he hadn't been to a church service since his schooldays and his knowledge of English hymnology was scant, to say the least. So what was it about this particular hymn that was stirring something long ago buried in the dim recesses of his mind? He stood holding the handle, ready to push the door shut, yet unable to move. Then it came to him. *He knew that hymn!* He'd sung it as a child himself. It had been the portal through which he'd passed into a realm in which he'd found a treasure he knew even then that he'd been seeking all his short life – *words*. Those intriguing marks on the page, those fascinating sounds on the air. Words, words, words. Words that even when he couldn't fully grasp their meaning still took hold of him and held him in their spell.

For the first time in more than sixty years he listened to those words again that had captivated him as a child in the morning assembly at Bellmill Primary:

> By cool Siloam's shady rill,
> How fair the lily grows!
> How sweet the breath, beneath the hill,
> Of Sharon's dewy rose.

He was aware of someone touching his arm and he turned his head to see the waitress standing next to him and looking concerned.

'Mr Gold, are you alright?' There was a note of genuine anxiety in her voice. 'Do you need some help?'

'Nnno. I'm OK,' he responded, shaking his head and brushing her hand brusquely from his arm. 'It's j-j-just that sssong. It reminded m-m-me of something. A long time ago... It d-d-doesn't mmmatter.'

He walked back to his table and sat down, embarrassed at the attention he'd drawn to himself and angry that he'd allowed something to breach the barrier he'd carefully constructed around his memories and emotions. He poured a second cup of tea and tried to pretend that nothing had happened. But something *had* happened. It was impossible to ignore it, and it was threatening to make him cry. He wiped his face with the serviette and hoped that no one had seen the tear that was trickling slowly down his cheek. Several more customers had just come in and were taking up the attention of the waitress. And the elderly stranger sitting by the window was struggling to his feet and getting ready to leave. He breathed a sigh of relief. No one else had witnessed what had taken place a few minutes before. He was safe from any further unwanted interest.

When the old man on the other side of the room eventually managed to get to his feet, however, he didn't leave. Instead, he shuffled his way across, leaning forward at a precarious angle that made Matthew think he might fall over at any moment.

'Do you mind if I join you, Mr Gold?' he asked almost in a whisper as he reached the table.

The request took Matthew by surprise, and, before he could reply, his uninvited guest had lowered himself into the chair opposite.

'Forgive my intrusion. My name's Sam Andrews. I'm waiting for my son. His youngest boy's in the choir you can hear practising in the church. He's coming to pick us both up at lunchtime when they've finished their rehearsal. But please say if you want me to leave you alone.'

He looked at Matthew and, since no immediate response came, he took that as permission to continue.

'Correct me if I'm wrong, but you are Matthew Gold, aren't you? I mean *the* Matthew Gold. I'm an admirer of your work. I still have to keep reminding myself that Matt Gee was a pseudonym.' He gave a croaky chuckle and a slow smile spread across his otherwise impassive features. 'I always felt that there was more to your writing than what was on the page, if you take my meaning. I suspect we all want to be like your Monty Silver – finding out the answers to life's mysteries.'

This wasn't what Matthew had expected. His first thought – one that he'd dismissed only out of respect for the man's age and sympathy for his physical frailty – had been to tell him to mind his own business. But it had been years since he'd received this kind of adulation from an admiring reader and it was more gratifying than he would have been willing to confess. He'd allow him another minute and then excuse himself and leave. His new-found companion leaned across the table and spoke even more quietly.

'I couldn't help overhearing your conversation with the waitress over by the door. I'm not as alert as I once was. Parkinson's, of course. You'll have noticed that, I'm sure. But unless I'm very much mistaken, that was a more significant moment than you were letting on...'

Matthew could feel the irritation rising in him. Now the man was meddling and it was time to bring the conversation to an end. Not wanting to attract any further attention to himself, he decided to politely thank him for his concern, tell him that he didn't wish to speak about it, and leave as quickly as possible. But the evocative sound of children's voices singing the strange old hymn that he'd once loved had triggered a seismic upheaval deep within him and released a tsunami of long-suppressed feelings. And the fissure it caused in the wall he'd built up over so many years was deeper and wider than he knew. As the memories and emotions flooded over him, he could no longer obey what his conscious mind was trying to tell him. What he said was not what he'd intended to say.

'Yyyes, it was,' he admitted. 'It t-t-took mmme back to mmmy childhood. We used t-t-to sing that hymn in assem-assem-assembly.'

Sam Andrews chuckled again and laid the palms of his hands on the table to stop them from trembling.

'Hmm… those old hymns can do that to me too. And that's a strange one. I never knew what it meant when I was a lad. Not sure that I understand that first verse even now. There weren't too many shady rills and dewy roses where I grew up. But it gets hold of you, even if you've no idea what it means.'

Smiling at strangers was not something Matthew did regularly. But he smiled at Sam's words, amused and pleased, to a degree he couldn't really understand, at the discovery of another human being on whom a sentimental melody and four lines of fairly mediocre poetry had had a similar effect.

'I'd be willing to wager,' Sam mused as he looked around, 'that we're the only people in this tearoom who know that hymn. I was surprised when I heard Finn tell his dad that the choir were including it in their concert. I hadn't heard anyone sing it for years. Do you know all the verses?'

Matthew confessed that he knew only the first four lines and that, as far as he could recall, they'd never got beyond the first verse in his school.

'That's not really surprising. By verse two it's fairly clear that dear old Bishop Reginald Heber who wrote it back in the early 1800s was trying to paint a word-picture of the perfect childhood. But then it gets a lot darker. Listen…'

Sam beckoned to Matthew to lean forward and began to sing very quietly and surprisingly tunefully:

> By cool Siloam's shady rill
> The lily must decay;
> The rose that blooms beneath the hill
> Must shortly fade away.
>
> And soon, too soon, the wintry hour
> Of man's maturer age
> Will shake the soul with sorrow's power
> And stormy passion's rage.

'They used to make us sing those verses in my old school as ten-year-olds.' Sam was smiling and chuckling again, and it seemed to Matthew he did that surprisingly often for a man in his condition. 'All that stuff about decaying flowers and wintry hours was way over the heads of us kids. And that was no bad thing. I still don't think it's suitable for children. Though now I'm in my ninth decade I think I've learned a bit about life's stormy passions and raging sorrows. Old-fashioned language, no doubt, but true all the same. And I sometimes wonder if we live in a culture where we've forgotten how to talk about the hard stuff that everybody has to face at some time in their life.'

The smile faded and Sam took a deep breath. He was looking intently at Matthew.

'I'm pretty sure that you've had your share of passions and sorrows, Mr Gold. It's a few years ago now, but I remember reading about the tragic air accident that took the lives of your publishers. I think I read at the time that they'd become your friends. That couldn't have been easy, I'm guessing…'

Quite how someone who was affected by the tremors of Parkinson's disease could hold such a steady stare, Matthew couldn't work out. But short of closing his eyes or getting up and walking out, he couldn't escape the penetrating gaze of the man sitting on the other side of the table. He suspected it would pierce through any smokescreen of generalities or evasive talk he might try to hide behind.

'Let me order another pot of tea,' Sam suggested. 'I noticed you're an Earl Grey man like myself. We've got about an hour before my son gets here. That gives us time for some proper conversation.'

When he looked back on that morning, Matthew struggled to explain how a man he'd never met before, without leaving him feeling coerced or manipulated, had got him to the place where he began to speak about himself with an honesty and at a depth he'd never done before. He talked a lot, cried a little and laughed more than he'd done in a long time, while Sam Andrews listened and interrupted only when he needed him to explain something a little more fully. It was almost twelve noon when their conversation began to draw to a conclusion.

'Nnnow I've t-t-told you mmmore about mmmyself,' Matthew confessed, 'than I've ever t-t-told anyone else.'

'It's been a privilege to hear your story,' Sam responded with another hoarse chuckle. 'And I think now I understand a little better why I found those *Monty Silver Mysteries* so interesting. I'm guessing that writing's been much more to you than just a way of earning a living...'

The door opened at that moment and a tall man came into the tearoom with a very small boy by his side. The boy looked around for a second or two, let go of the man's hand and ran across the room calling out in a sing-song kind of voice, 'Grrrampa!' Sam stopped mid-sentence and waited for him. The man who'd brought the boy to the door, whom Matthew correctly assumed to be one of the adults from the choir rehearsal, waved and left the boy in the care of his grandfather.

'Finn,' Sam said as the boy climbed onto his knee, 'this gentleman is Mr Gold. He likes the same kind of tea as Grampa and he's a famous writer. And, Mr Gold, this is Finn Andrews. He's seven and a quarter, he doesn't like tea, but he *does* like singing and he loves ice cream. And his dad told me this morning that it was OK for me to order an ice cream sundae for my boy who must be in need of refreshment after all that singing. But first, Finn, shake hands with Mr Gold and introduce yourself.'

The boy slipped down from his grandfather's knee. He held out his hand to Matthew and took two deep breaths.

'It's n-n-nice to mmmeet you, Mmmr G-G-Gold. I'm Fffinn Andrews.'

Matthew couldn't distinguish whether the noise he heard was just someone's chair scraping on the floor or whether Sam had given a momentary chuckle. There was a lump in his throat as he took the boy's hand in his.

'And I'm Mmmatthew G-G-Gold. And it's v-v-very nice t-t-to mmmeet you, too.'

The waitress brought over an extra chair for Finn, who was looking very pleased with himself, and Sam ordered a third pot of tea and the promised ice cream sundae before addressing his grandson again.

'Finn, this is the very first time I've met Mr Gold. He's a very interesting man. And he's someone you can take encouragement from. He's been telling me that when he was a little boy there were unkind people who made fun of *his* stammer. Now, what was that word you and I talked about the other day to describe someone who sets us an example and encourages us?'

The boy thought for a moment. 'I knnnow. An inspi-inspi-inspiration,' he announced proudly, his look of intense concentration changing to one of sheer triumph. His reward was a hug from his grandfather, another handshake from Matthew, and an ice cream sundae that then took up all his attention, leaving the two men free to finish their conversation.

'I hope I haven't embarrassed you,' Sam said apologetically. He fumbled with trembling hands for his pen, carefully wrote down his phone number in tiny letters, and gave it to Matthew. 'I really should learn to mind my own business, but it was when I overheard your conversation with the waitress over by the door that I twigged who you must be and I remembered reading that you've lived with a stammer throughout your life. I wanted to talk to you for myself and I also wanted my grandson to meet you. He's a bright kid, but he's faced some bullying from a bigger lad at school and it's shaken his confidence a little. It's good for him to meet older folk who've had the same struggles and learned to cope. You really have been an inspiration to him. And to me.'

The irony for Matthew was that for almost the only time in his life, his 'stupid stammer', as he'd so often described it to himself, hadn't been an embarrassment. Well, it was. But not *only* an embarrassment. Maybe not even *mainly* an embarrassment. It was just – just what? It was still a nuisance, still something he'd rather be without, still an impediment that got in the way and frustrated him. But as he talked with Sam Andrews it was just part of who he was, a thing he had to live with. Like some people are short-sighted, or hard of hearing, or have a funny twitch or a big nose, or any one of a thousand different imperfections. Sam hadn't given him any counselling and didn't offer him any therapy. All he'd done was to speak with him as a fellow human being. And, just as he wouldn't dream of apologising for his Parkinson's or want anybody to feel sorry for him, he didn't expect Matthew to apologise for his stammer or consider him to be someone deserving of his pity. In fact, he saw him as an inspiration!

For so many years, his birthday had passed as just another unremarkable day. And even though he'd reached the age of seventy, he'd got up that morning with no intention of marking what others would have seen as a significant milestone in life. It had, however, turned out to be a quite remarkable day, unlike any other, and one that he would not easily forget. The last thing he'd imagined when he'd set out that morning was that he'd meet a little boy who'd remind him so much of himself at that age. A little boy with a stammer who called his grandfather 'Grampa' and whose grandfather referred to him as 'my boy'. What were the chances of that happening? And what, if anything, should he make of it? If he didn't know better, if life hadn't given him so many hard knocks, he might have wondered if a coincidence like that was part of the mystery to which he'd been trying to find a solution for so long. Or even one of those missing pages that had troubled his dreams for so many years…

chapter 28
2017

The piece of paper with the phone number scribbled on it in the neat and tiny handwriting characteristic of a writer with Parkinson's disease lay on the counter under the clock on the wall in Matthew's kitchen. As its glowing red digital lettering marked the unrelenting passing of the days, he looked at that piece of paper from time to time and thought about calling Sam Andrews. And each time he pushed it away again. He'd always hated using the phone because of his stammer, and it was so long since he'd taken the initiative in contacting anyone that he couldn't summon up the willpower to pick up the receiver. But three weeks after their meeting on his seventieth birthday, having managed to overcome his reluctance, he'd made the call. Now he was sitting at his usual table in The Sanctuary Tearoom and waiting nervously. He didn't have to wait long. At exactly 10.15, as they'd agreed, the door opened and Sam came walking slowly towards him. It took Matthew by surprise just how glad he was to see him again.

It was the first of what became regular monthly encounters through the spring and summer of 2017. There was never any set agenda for their meetings, and often Matthew would have been hard pressed to remember in detail exactly what they'd talked about. But that, he gradually began to realise, was one of the reasons he looked forward so much to their conversations. Rather than finding solutions to troubling questions as he'd anticipated, he was rediscovering the simple pleasure of human company. He tried to explain to Sam on one occasion why he found their times together so helpful. The best he could come up with was to say that while he wasn't arriving at any answers, it felt like he was embarking on an odyssey – a journey to places he'd either forgotten or had never known existed, and one that would take the rest of his life. That brought one of Sam's throaty chuckles, and he'd added enigmatically, 'And then some, and then some.'

As the months passed, Matthew learned to his considerable surprise that Sam was a retired clergyman who'd spent most of his career teaching in theological colleges, mainly in the north-west of the country. Apart from the funerals he'd attended, Matthew had difficulty recalling any occasion on which he'd come within a yard of a minister of religion. And this man certainly didn't fit his stereotypical image of a man of the cloth. It was from odd snippets of their conversations, however, that he began to form an impression that Sam's great passion in life went far beyond the academic mentoring of his students. He seemed to have been blessed with an uncanny ability to turn up in the lives of all kinds of people seemingly from out of the blue, stay as long as they needed him and then, when his work was done, quietly leave as suddenly as he'd arrived. And, as that picture took shape in his mind, it brought with it a growing awareness that his time with this man who'd arrived unexpectedly in his life might be limited. He was always relieved at the end of each of their meetings when Sam would glance at the clock and say, 'Shall we meet next month?'

The pattern for their meetings had become well established by their September appointment. Matthew, who always got to The Sanctuary Tearoom at precisely 10.15, ordered their tea and scones, and settled himself at what had become 'their table'. Sam, who depended on a friendly neighbour or one of his sons to drop him off, usually arrived a few minutes later. At 10.20 the door opened and Matthew got up to greet the person whose company had come to mean so much to him. But it wasn't Sam who came through the door. It was his younger son, Ian, whom Matthew had met briefly when he'd brought his father a couple of months before. He greeted Matthew and sat down on the chair opposite, where his father usually sat.

'Mr Gold, I've got some bad news, though my dad would be annoyed with me for describing it in that way.' From the expression on his face, it wasn't difficult for Matthew to guess what he was about to hear. 'Dad died yesterday morning. The hospital diagnosed a very aggressive form of cancer a few months ago and he knew he didn't have long. We didn't expect the end to come so quick, but his condition deteriorated rapidly over the last few days. He was adamant that I should deliver this to you by hand if he didn't make it. He wrote it just last week.

It was one of the last things he did before he lost consciousness.'

Ian Andrews unzipped the leather bag he was carrying and took out a sealed white envelope, which he slid gently across the table. Matthew picked up a knife, wiped it carefully with his serviette to make sure it was clean, and slit the envelope open. He eased the letter out and unfolded it on the table in front of him. Ian suggested that perhaps he should leave him alone, but Matthew indicated that he wanted him to stay while he read it. It was written in that same neat and tiny handwriting that had been on the piece of paper Sam had given him with his phone number when they'd first met.

Dear Matthew,

As I'm writing this letter, I can picture you reading it in The Sanctuary Tearoom. Thank you for the great times we've had there in the few months we've known each other.

Looking back on my life, I think that I've probably been too ready to give people the benefit of my advice. (My wife used to tell me that often. And my sons continue to remind me that it's a fault that continues with me into old age!) But even old men can learn to do better. So I've tried very hard in our conversations to do a lot more listening than talking, and I hope that's been helpful to you. The fact that you're reading this now means, of course, that I've died. So, I hope you won't mind me saying some things to you that I would have liked to have said face to face if we'd had more time. The benefit of doing it this way is that unlike one of our conversations, where you would have been too polite to stop an old man in mid-sentence, you can fold this letter up and stick it back in the envelope – or even throw it away – if you think that in my confused state I'm writing nonsense without realising it!

Unsurprisingly, given that you're a writer of detective novels, the word 'mystery' has cropped up more than a few times when we've been talking to each other. I know that for you, it's a BIG word that brings together all the pain and suffering of the world in which we live. And I know, too, that you've honestly and courageously tried to find answers that will go some way to explaining the mystery at the very heart of things.

Though we haven't talked too much about it, you'll have gleaned from our chats that I'm – to use a phrase I heartily dislike – a religious man. Sometimes religious folk like me can fall into the trap of thinking that we've solved the mystery and that we've got all the answers, if only we can get people to listen to us and to accept them. And I suspect that that way of thinking has allowed well-meaning and sincere individuals to do a lot of damage, both to their own faith and to other people. The older – and, hopefully the wiser – I have become, the more I have moved away from that way of thinking.

Here's the truth as I see it. It's the truth that lies at the very heart of the faith I'm having to hold on to so tenaciously at this moment, and which I've tried to live by, albeit imperfectly, throughout my life.

The mystery confronts all of us every day of our lives. Cruelty and pain are somehow intertwined with *the very warp and woof of the universe. They will go on distorting the pattern of truth and beauty that we still manage to discern, despite their presence, as long as this present world order continues.*

The question as to how and why they got there is one we have to live with. Neither religion nor philosophy has a complete and final answer. It remains a mystery.

But there is a greater mystery – one that I believe is deeper and stronger than the mystery of evil and suffering. And that deeper mystery is this: when someone willingly takes the pain and suffering around them upon themselves, refuses to be beaten or contaminated by it, a wonderful and unexpected transformation takes place. Healing appears where there is hurt, beauty appears where there is ugliness, joy appears where there is misery, forgiveness appears where there is bitterness, love appears where there is hate, good appears where there is evil.

Even as I face the prospect of dying, I'm willing to stake my life on that, Matthew. And if the story my faith is built on is true, Someone once did that – literally staked His life on it – to a degree and to a depth that no one else has ever been able to do. Such was the impact of the risk He had to take and the price He had to pay that it gives me hope that one day the mystery will be clear and plain and the perfect pattern of creation will be restored and revealed.

But there I go again – falling back into my old habits, preaching and telling other people what to believe! You'll have to find it out for yourself, make up your own mind as to whether what I've said is the truth or just the muddled ramblings of a dying man who's peeved about the possibility of missing tea and scones with his pal. But if I'm right, you can be sure that even while you're reading this letter, I'll be mentioning your name in the highest circles. But that's another mystery!

Go deep, Matthew, and take the risk.

Always your friend,

Sam Andrews

PS I've given Ian, my son, the money to pay the waitress. Make sure he doesn't slip off without paying. He's been doing that since he was a kid! This one's on me.

When he got to the end of the letter, Matthew pushed it to one side to avoid his tears spilling on to it and making the ink run. He wiped his eyes and looked at Ian, who was reaching for his wallet.

'I don't know what the rest of the letter says, but he did read me the PS at the end. I'm not about to disobey his instructions.' He chuckled in a way that reminded Matthew of Sam. 'He'd haunt me for the rest of my days if I walked out of here without paying.'

It was only when they'd stopped laughing together at Ian's words that they realised The Sanctuary Tearoom had gone quiet. Everyone else in the place, most of whom had got to know Sam from his visits, was watching them, having either overheard or guessed the news that Ian Andrews had been sharing. Matthew summoned the waitress.

'P-p-please b-b-bring mmmy order. Sssam would b-b-be mmmore than annoyed if he thought wwwe'd wwwasted a p-p-pot of Earl G-g-grey tea. And mmmake sure everyb-b-body else has a fffull c-c-cup.'

Five minutes later, eleven other regulars of The Sanctuary Tearoom stood with Matthew Gold and Ian Andrews and raised their tea and coffee cups as Matthew proposed a toast. He wasn't going to let his stammer stop him from doing this. He took two deep breaths and said:

'S-S-Sam Andrews. A wwwise and g-g-good fffriend.'

chapter 29

2017

Sam Andrews' funeral took place in a crowded church in the centre of Manchester on Friday 29th September, a day in which clouds and sunshine constantly gave way to each other. It was unlike any other that Matthew had ever attended. There was, as he'd expected, a dignified solemnity in the service and tears on the faces of the more than 1,000 people seated in the church and the nearly 500 who stood outside and watched the proceedings relayed on a large screen that had been set up for the occasion. But there was also a sense of joy – you might even describe it as fun, Matthew noted to his surprise – and a great deal of laughter. He had the distinct impression from what was said in the service and from the conversations he overheard afterwards that at least half the people there had benefited from Sam's insight and companionship at some time in their lives.

The service was led by an Anglican vicar, the Reverend Pippa Sheppard, a young married woman with two school-age children. She told the congregation that Sam had turned up when she was in the middle of a crisis that had impacted not only her family and her church, but also the surrounding community. Without him walking alongside her at that time, she acknowledged, she'd no idea how she would have come through it. One of the lessons was read by an arty-looking man in his seventies, dressed in a cardigan, checked shirt and corduroy trousers. The respectful silence that fell on the church as he walked to the lectern was broken by a combination of laughter and applause when he prefaced the reading by declaring that although he'd acquired a certain notoriety for burgling churches, he had, in fact, done it only once. Most surprising of all to Matthew was the participation of a father and son who were announced simply as Ray and Ollie and initially sounded like some kind of double act. Ray explained that he was a preacher turned relationship counsellor trying to help others avoid the kind of mistakes he'd made in the past. Ollie introduced himself as a stand-up comic who spent most of his life trying to get people he'd never met before to like him enough to laugh at his jokes. It was, Matthew was absolutely certain, the first time that he'd ever heard a series of one-liners delivered to an enthusiastic audience at a funeral service. The hilarity subsided very quickly when they spoke of the family tragedy that might have destroyed their relationship had Sam not arrived on the scene with his supportive friendship and robust wisdom.

Matthew noticed that there were one or two people who glanced in his direction, probably remembering him from an old newspaper photograph, he guessed, and thinking that he looked vaguely familiar. But he was glad to be unrecognised and to be able to confine his conversations with people he didn't know to a few polite words of greeting. It was only when he was leaving the church, having shaken hands with Sam's sons and thanked them for inviting him to the service, that he spotted a woman hurrying towards him. She was around his age, of slight build, smartly but unfussily dressed, and her short white hair retained the reddish tinge of what he assumed had been her original colouring. The closer she came, the clearer it became that she was determined to speak to him.

'Well, well, well. After all these years...' She grinned and shook her head in disbelief. 'You *must* be Matthew Gold. Please tell me I'm right.'

Over the years he'd met more than a few unbalanced people for whom a normal interest in crime fiction had developed into a fanatical obsession with a particular story or an unhealthy fixation on one of the main characters. He'd learned that they could turn up in the most unlikely places. This woman didn't seem to fit the typical profile, but you could never be sure. Ignoring her or pretending he was someone else, however, might just serve to make her all the more persistent and result in a scene that would be highly inappropriate at the end of a funeral service. He nodded in agreement that he was indeed who she thought he was, hoping that she might settle for an autograph or a selfie and leave him alone. He was totally unprepared for what happened next.

'I'm so pleased to see you again!' she exclaimed, throwing her arms around him and planting a kiss on his cheek. 'I've thought about you a lot over the years when I've seen your photograph and read stuff about you in the newspapers. Read some of your books too. Even thought about trying to get in touch. Never expected to see you here, though. I'll bet you can't remember the last time we spoke to each other.'

His embarrassment increasing by the minute, he shook his head and confessed that he neither recognised her nor recalled the occasion.

'Well, let me remind you,' she said, laughing and releasing him from her hold. 'Bellmill Primary School? Nearly sixty years ago?'

He shook his head, still none the wiser for her prompting.

'It was a filthy wet day,' she said, her eyes lighting up at the memory. 'You were wearing football boots, you were covered in mud, and I was standing waiting for you on the path. I wanted to congratulate you on scoring the winning goal and tell you how much I admired the way you dealt with Danny Johnstone and his gang.'

Now it was Matthew's turn to laugh as he searched his memory for the name of the ginger-haired girl with the prominent teeth who'd made him blush such a long time ago.

'You mmmust b-b-be... Elsie B-B-Brownlee! I'd forgo-forgotten all about that. How on earth d-d-do yyyou rrremember it so c-c-clearly?'

'You still don't get it, do you?' She was shaking her head and laughing again. 'That's men for you! I remember it so clearly because I had such a crush on you. I thought you were clever and nice-looking and brave. *You were my hero.* My first great passion, even though my love, alas, was unrecognised and unrequited. That's why I remember it so clearly. If you'd been a bit more on the ball coming off that football field – no pun intended – I might have been Mrs Elsie Gold now, instead of Mrs Elsie Ratcliffe.'

He was seventy years of age, a successful writer, wearing an expensive suit, but, just like the eleven-year-old boy in the muddy, wet football strip, he was blushing and completely stuck for words. And just as she'd done back in 1958, Elsie rescued him from his awkward silence.

'We can't stand here all day. They'll be throwing us out of the church if we don't move. But I'd love to chat. Are you dashing off somewhere? Or have you got time for a coffee?'

Matthew explained that he hadn't driven since he'd had a near miss on the A9 in Scotland getting on for twenty years before and that a taxi would be coming in fifteen minutes to take him home. But she persuaded him, without too much difficulty, to cancel the booking, and less than half an hour later they were getting out of her car and walking into The Sanctuary Tearoom together. He'd insisted on coming here rather than going to one of the many coffee shops in Manchester, where he knew from experience it was impossible to get a proper cup of tea. On their drive from the city centre, being careful to avoid going into too many details, he'd sketched the broad outline of his life until his chance encounter with Sam Andrews. And when they were settled at his favourite table – the one where he'd always sat with Sam – he listened while Elsie animatedly filled him in on her story since last they'd met.

'We moved back to England, you might remember. I went to six different schools as my dad moved around with his work until I went back up to Scotland to study medicine at Edinburgh university. That's when I first met Sam Andrews. I heard him speak at a conference on medical ethics when I was a medical student and he made a big impression on me. I've kept in touch with him down through the years. I've contacted him whenever I've run into a tricky ethical issue or even a personal problem that I couldn't solve. He was great. He wouldn't ever give me the answer, but he wouldn't put up with any waffle. And he always made me think it through.'

Matthew nodded in agreement and commented on how surprised he was that one man could have had such an impact on so many people's lives over so many years. He was equally surprised, when Elsie took the opportunity to replenish her cup from the coffee pot on the table, that someone could drink as much black coffee as she was managing to do over such a short space of time. But he thought it better to keep those thoughts to himself. For a sedate tea drinker to upset a woman as formidable as this one, especially when her intake of so much caffeine was resulting in such an adrenaline rush, didn't seem like a good idea. He contented himself with waiting for her to continue.

'I joined a GP practice in Birmingham, and that's where I met Arthur, my husband. He was a window cleaner. Cleaned the windows at the surgery. My folks weren't too happy about it. Thought that after all they'd put into my education I was marrying beneath my station. They were wrong. He was a good man. Lived the life he loved and loved the life he lived. We had a great marriage, more than thirty years together. Ten years now since he died. I've got a daughter living over in the States, married with two young kids. She's a lawyer. My son lives in London with his partner. He's got a market stall selling fruit and veg. He's very like his dad, loves to be out of doors and be his own boss. We're a close family without needing to be close, if you know what I mean. And that leaves me free pretty much to please myself and keep active.'

'So I g-g-guess it's g-g-golf in the mmmornings, long wwwalks in the afternoon, and b-b-bridge with your ffffriends in the evening,' Matthew chipped in while Elsie paused just long enough to drain her cup and fill it again. She dismissed his vain attempt at humour contemptuously.

'Oh no, that's not for me,' she retorted, rolling her eyes in disgust at the prospect of what she obviously considered to be a life of pointless ease. 'No, I'm still well and fit and I've got enough money to be comfortable. I want to keep doing something useful with the active years I've got ahead of me. I want to use the hard-earned skills I've got to do some good. If I ever manage to justify taking up space in the world it's all down to these…'

She stopped speaking and flashed an exaggerated smile that displayed her perfectly straight white teeth. Matthew responded with a questioning look that prompted her to explain more precisely what she meant.

'I don't know if you remember, but I when I was a kid, I had ginger hair and prominent teeth. I didn't mind so much being called "gingernut". In fact, the older I've got the more I like my colouring, especially now that it gives a bit of contrast to my white hair. But "buck teeth" used to really upset me. I cried a lot about that. My folks didn't really know about orthodontics back then. It wasn't until I was in my mid-teens that I had it fixed and it made such a difference to my confidence. I wanted to smile at everybody I met for the first little while. People must have thought I was crazy.'

She smiled momentarily to herself as she recalled the pleasure her corrected teeth had given her. Then, realising that Matthew still couldn't work out why her dental treatment had proved to be as important as she'd indicated, she went on with her explanation.

'There were a number of Traveller families in the area of Birmingham where our surgery was situated. Because of their itinerant way of life, it wasn't always easy for them to access the medical care they needed. During my first year in the practice, a young mum came in one day with her six-year-old little girl. It still brings tears to my eyes to think about that child. She had a very severe cleft palate, which hadn't been treated at all. Back then, there were even some doctors who would still refer to it as a "hare lip". It was a horrible expression and thankfully you don't hear it very often now. The family had decided to settle in the city and they'd found a school where the head understood their culture and worked hard to accommodate their children. But this youngster was getting bullied because of her appearance and she was refusing to go to school. Her mum was at her wits' end. She had two other kids, and just making ends meet was hard enough without this.

'Just thinking about my own childhood made me feel really sorry for the little girl. Having prominent teeth like I had as a kid was nowhere near as bad as what she had to deal with. But at least I had some idea of what she was going through with the bullying, and I understood her embarrassment about how she looked. I made up my mind to do something about it. We were able to refer them to a local hospital, where they carried out the surgery and linked them up with ongoing dental care and speech therapy. The difference it made to the little girl and the entire family made me realise why I'd gone into medicine.'

Matthew acknowledged that he could understand how her own experience as a child had given her an ability to empathise with others facing similar situations. But Elsie had more to tell. The experience had been life-changing for her as well as for her youthful patient.

'That little Traveller girl made a lasting impression on me. I couldn't get her out of my mind, and after three years in general practice I went back to medical school and trained as a plastic surgeon specialising in cleft palate surgery. By then I'd met and married my husband and we'd just had our first child. So the timing wasn't ideal. But Arthur was great. He supported my decision, kept his window cleaning business going, brought up our daughter almost single-handed and looked after the house while I qualified. It was hard at the time, but it was the best decision I ever made. And that's what I've done since then. I've lost count of how many kids I've operated on, but I never lose the thrill of seeing the transformation that surgery makes, not just to their appearance but to the rest of their lives.'

There was a look of satisfaction on Elsie's face as she reached what Matthew assumed was the climax of her story. It was, he thought, an appropriate point at which to make a suitable interjection.

'You *hhhave* had an inter-interesting life.'

His comment served only to remind Elsie that what had encouraged her to launch into her story was that he'd had the temerity to suggest that she'd settled down to a comfortable retirement.

'Oh, it's not over yet. Not by any means. I've officially retired from the NHS. But that means I'm free to give my services to a charity working overseas in poorer countries to train and equip local doctors and healthcare workers to provide cleft repair surgery and aftercare to children and young people who would otherwise have to live with the condition. If we can get these kids operated on in the first year or two of life it makes all the difference to their future. I spend about six months abroad each year, and I've no intention of settling into my armchair as long as I've got health and strength and good strong coffee to keep me stimulated and wide awake.'

Her conclusion to her summary of her life reminded her that the she'd drained the coffee pot. She summoned the waitress, asked for a replacement and then threw out a question.

'So what about you, Matthew? You look fit and healthy. What are you up to now? I'm guessing that you're still writing…'

It was a question he'd been dreading. This woman's intentional and active involvement was in stark contrast to his own deliberate and reclusive withdrawal from the world. It wasn't that she didn't think about things or that she chose to ignore the fact that life was often unfair and unkind to people. Undeniably, from what she'd said, those things touched her deeply. Like him, she was confronted by the mystery of life. But in the face of the apparently meaningless suffering inflicted on unsuspecting humans by sheer blind chance, her response was to stare it in the face defiantly, roll up her sleeves and do something. He was both envious of her resolve and embarrassed by his own retreat. She at least had a partial answer. He still had none.

'I'm afraid I'm nnnot d-d-oing mmmuch of anything,' he confessed. 'It all g-g-got a b-b-bit too mmuch for me. I mmmore or less k-k-keep myself to myself these d-d-days.'

He lifted his head and glanced across the table, half-expecting a look of pity or even contempt. What he actually observed was an expression that suggested a much more complex reaction.

'Oh Matthew, I know that urge to run away and hide all too well.' Her voice was quieter and she was speaking more slowly than before. 'I guess the difference between you and me is that you have a kind of courage I don't have. I wouldn't dare to stop and think about what it all means. If I did, I've no idea what it would do to me. Maybe that's why I keep going like I do. People sometimes tell me how brave I am. Somebody even put my name up for an honour, but I soon put a stop to that. I'd feel a complete fraud accepting an OBE or whatever. I'm no kind of hero. The best I can hope for is to do a little bit of good and keep my conscience clear. The rest is a mystery to me.'

They sat in silence for a time. The pot of fresh coffee was left untouched. Elsie leaned back in her chair and Matthew rested his face in his hands. Neither of them noticed the waitress approach.

'Excuse me,' she said very softly, 'but we're closing in five minutes. Do you mind if I clear your table and give you your bill?'

'Of course not.' Elsie quickly reverted to her earlier breezy, confident manner. 'Time we were going anyway. I've got a two-hour drive home on the M6. Matthew tells me this is a regular haunt of his, so I'll let him be a gentleman and pay.'

The bill having been paid, they left The Sanctuary Tearoom and walked together without speaking, each lost in their thoughts, until they reached Elsie's car.

'Well, it's been wonderful to see you, Matthew,' she said, reaching into the bag that was slung over her shoulder. 'Here's my card. Let's keep in touch. For old time's sake, if nothing else.'

'I'd like that,' Matthew replied, unsure as to how truthful his words really were.

They hugged each other briefly, Elsie got into her car and drove the 100 miles south, and Matthew walked the two miles to his house. It was the end of a day of contrasts. The funeral of a friend he'd known for only six months and an unexpected meeting with someone he hadn't seen for sixty years. A church filled with music and memories and a one-to-one conversation with an old classmate he could only just recall. For a man to whom anything more than superficial human contact required a considerable effort, it had been an exhausting day. He went to bed earlier than usual that night and fell asleep almost instantly. By four o'clock in the morning, however, he was wide awake, his sleep disturbed by an all-too-familiar nightmare. One in which he was picking up the scattered sheets of a typed manuscript and trying to put them in some kind of order. But there were still three pages missing, the ones that would make sense of the story.

chapter 30
2017

The morning after Sam Andrews' funeral and his unexpected meeting with Elsie Ratcliffe, Matthew had a disturbing sense of anticlimax. It had felt at the time that it might well prove to be a significant day, but now that he was back in what had become the predictable and uneventful routine of his life, he was at a loss to know what to make of all that had happened in the last twenty-four hours. The fact that he'd been awake since four o'clock merely added to the irritability and restlessness he was feeling, and made it impossible for him to settle his mind to anything.

He was relieved when the red digital lettering of the clock on his kitchen wall showed that the time had reached 9.43. He waited precisely another two minutes before following his long-established practice and setting off for The Sanctuary Tearoom at 9.45. He'd made the walk so often that he didn't have to think about the route he was taking. As he settled into the steady rhythm of his steps, he would allow his mind to go blank, give himself permission to think of nothing and find a brief respite from the thoughts that sometimes threatened to trouble his waking hours almost as much as his dreams disturbed his sleep. Today, however, much to his annoyance, he was unusually distracted. He found himself taking a wrong turning and having to retrace his steps. By the time he was back on the right path he was so exasperated by his stupid mistake and by the way he was feeling that he turned back and headed home. His sudden decision to break out of his strict routine served only to increase his irritation. What on earth was going on with him?

As soon as he got home, he made himself a pot of tea and sat quietly in his kitchen trying to think his way through his confusion. Surely, he *had* to be right. His life might be considered dull by anyone who didn't really know him, but for nigh on twenty years its sheltering predictability had granted him the protection he'd sought from what a far greater writer than he was had perfectly described as 'the slings and arrows of outrageous fortune'. Elsie Ratcliffe might be prepared to risk everything in doing battle with the pain and suffering she saw around her. Her courage and tenacity were admirable, but plainly she didn't understand the enormity of the mystery, the moral and spiritual black hole at the heart of life that would ultimately absorb and destroy everything and everyone, good and bad alike.

But what if Sam was right? What if there really *was* something deeper, a greater mystery? What if Elsie wasn't just being courageous? What if she wasn't simply taking a foolhardy risk? What if she was actually reaching out, albeit unknowingly, and touching the edge of the deeper mystery where – he could remember Sam's words – hurts are healed, where ugliness is cleansed by beauty, where misery turns to joy, where bitterness becomes forgiveness, where hate is overcome by love and where evil is finally conquered by good? Only someone who'd actually gone there could ever know if it was true, could ever know that the deeper mystery was really there and not merely the product of misguided piety and an over-optimistic imagination.

And what if you left it too late because you were just too afraid or too self-absorbed or too wrapped up in something to take the risk? What if one day you *knew* – *knew* it in your heart the way you sometimes know things at a level beyond cold logic or mere rational thought – *knew*, or at least suspected or hoped, that the deeper mystery really was there, just waiting to be glimpsed and touched? What if one day you *knew*, but you'd left it too late to reach out? That would be the nightmare of the missing pages become a terrible reality. You'd never find the truth. You'd never reach any resolution of the mystery.

He smiled ruefully to himself. That recurring dream had imprinted itself so firmly on his mind. And it wasn't a helpful train of thought. Certainly not worth dwelling on. Better to resume his morning walk and clear his head of such negative thinking. He was just about to head back out of doors when something occurred to him, something that had been woken by those two words – *missing pages*. It had been lurking at the back of his mind for the last couple of weeks. He'd been going through some old papers in his desk drawer when he'd come across the two A4 pages that Bob Urquhart had given him when they'd met in Verricchia's Ice Cream Parlour – the pages that outlined his grandparents' involvement with the Bellmill Holiness and Bible Fellowship. They'd lain in the drawer untouched for the better part of twenty years. He'd scanned through them quickly before putting them back at the bottom of the pile. They brought back too many painful memories. But there was one paragraph that he couldn't get out of his head, though he couldn't bring to the forefront of his mind what it was about it that was troubling him.

He turned back, went into his study and opened the drawer. He found the two pages and read them again, more slowly and carefully this time. It didn't take him long to find the paragraph he was looking for. It was the second paragraph on the first page. The one that referred to the visit James Gold and Maggie Thompson had made to the cinema as teenagers on their first date:

She accepted his invitation to meet the following evening and agreed to keep their rendezvous a secret. James' intentions were entirely honourable and their conduct that evening was innocent – apart from two things. Maggie decided to let her long black hair down over her shoulders and James persuaded her that they should go to see a film in the Alhambra Picture House. Those two actions meant that they had breached the strict moral code of the Fellowship, which demanded that a woman should keep her hair neatly tied in a bun behind her head and forbade attendance at places of what they deemed to be 'worldly entertainment'. The elders of the Fellowship had long ago foreseen the temptation that would inevitably result from the touch of luxurious flowing hair on a young man, particularly in surroundings where the only light came from the flickering images of questionable conduct projected onto a cinema screen.

Reading those words again felt like a splinter that you might pick up without even realising it. You begin to feel it just beneath the surface of the skin; gradually your finger becomes uncomfortable, then inflamed, until eventually, if you don't remove it, it becomes a throbbing and festering sore. And the splinter that was lodged in his mind was that seemingly innocuous description of Maggie's decision to loosen the tightly coiled bun at the back of her head and allow her long black hair to fall over her shoulders. It must have been, Matthew imagined, an unpremeditated, maybe even unconscious, gesture of rebellion, an instinctive bid to free herself from the narrow confines of the legalistic cult with which her life had become entangled. *But almost certainly, she'd never dared to do it again.* Not after the public humiliation imposed on her as the discipline for their visit to the cinema. Not after facing the prospect of exclusion. For all its strict rules and stifling demands, the Bellmill Holiness and Bible Fellowship offered her a security she could not live without. Sweeping her hair from her face and gathering it at the back of her head every morning had become her daily sacrament of submission, the ritual re-enactment of her vow never again to risk stepping outside the boundaries of unquestioning certainty. In the sixteen years Matthew had lived in the same house as Maggie Gold, never once had he seen her with her hair down.

But why were those words continuing to throb in his mind, like a tiny but jagged shard hidden just out of sight and just beyond his reach? What was he failing to see? He stood by his desk, staring down at the page until in an instant an image he'd managed to shut out from his memory for more than half a century appeared with a sudden and vivid intensity and a sharpness of focus that made him gasp. It was 22nd November 1963 and he was back in 29C Liberty Court, peering through the partially open bedroom door. On the other side of the room he could see again his grandmother, lying unnaturally still and fully clothed on top of the bed. *Her grey hair, which she always kept swept back severely from her face and tied in a bun behind her head, was lying loose on the pillow.*

The boy in his mid-teens who'd first witnessed the sight had no knowledge of his grandparents' early life and no way of understanding the possible significance of that detail. The horror of the self-inflicted death he had witnessed was in itself more than he could comprehend. But for the man in his seventies in whose mind the tragic scene was being replayed, there were unsettling questions that he could not avoid. Why had Maggie Gold taken her own life when such a deed went against everything she had been taught? Had she been overcome by guilt at her hard-hearted self-righteousness? Was her suicide an escape from a life that was bereft of happiness? Or was it simply what, in our more enlightened age with its greater understanding of mental illness, we would describe as the consequence of an untreated debilitating depression?

But beyond everything else, there was one all-encompassing question that now presented itself and that he could not ignore. Why had the woman who had never again allowed her hair to fall on her shoulders since that far-off evening in the cinema, loosened it in her last moments before taking her own life? Was she remembering sitting beside James Gold in the darkened theatre and sensing for the first time the urge to open her life and give her love to another? Was her suicide at some deep subconscious level a recognition of the terrible truth that her religious devotion had been a wrong path, a dead-end road that separated her from others and led to nowhere? Had she realised too late, perhaps, that the rigid dogma to which she'd uncritically assented and the exacting morality to which she'd zealously adhered had become an elaborate and confusing maze, trapping her and keeping her from the call to love, the call to embrace the pain and suffering of others, the call to touch the edge of what Sam had called 'the deeper mystery' where healing and love and goodness were waiting to be found?

He could never know for sure. But the unexpected surfacing of a memory that had been smothered for so long brought with it uncomfortable truths that would not go away. His grandmother had been a woman in deep inner pain, pain that she'd hidden from everyone around her. Her grim piety and her harsh attitude to others had served to buttress the dam she'd constructed in an attempt to stem the tide of her deepest hopes and fears. It was a barrier that would ultimately be swept away in a deluge of remorse that would cost her her life. What was even more disturbing to him was the realisation that he was more like this woman he'd bitterly resented all his life than he'd been willing to acknowledge. If she had retreated into the graceless sanctuary of her religious certainties, he had taken refuge in the selfish security of his possessions. Just like his grandmother, he'd been overwhelmed by the mess and mystery of life. Just like her, he'd failed to find the courage to take the risk and to reach out to others. It left him with one final question that demanded an answer: had he, too, left it too late to respond to the call to touch the edge of what Sam had called 'the deeper mystery', where healing and love and goodness were waiting to be found?

chapter 31

2018

Matthew Gold was a very long way from home. Enjoying an al fresco dinner on a balmy August evening in a garden that clung precariously to the sloping surface of a mountain overlooking Rio de Janeiro, he felt even further from England than the 6,000 miles he'd flown the day before. Practised traveller though he was, this was something he'd never before experienced. Stretching below he could see what looked like endless houses rising organically out of the hillside, one on top of the other. And immediately around him was a riot of plants and herbs growing not only directly out of the soil, but dangling from the edge of the rooftop, hanging from window ledges and sprouting from the scores of glass jars that filled every unoccupied patch of ground. It had been almost impossible for him to believe that only fifteen years earlier this fertile oasis had been a foul-smelling, disease-ridden garbage tip, until he looked more closely and realised that almost everything around him that wasn't actually growing had been made out of the trash that had once filled the site. Old tyres, plastic bottles, discarded wheel rims and broken household utensils had all been recycled and adapted to some practical use and invested with a peculiar and captivating beauty in the process.

Such transformations were, he was discovering in the few hours he'd been here, the very life-blood that made survival possible in these townships. Over their *feijoada* – a warm stew of black beans, sausages and cuts of pork served with white rice – Lucas, a local community activist who'd generously offered to be both his host and his guide during his stay, had given him a quick lesson on the history of the Brazilian *favelas*. Back in the seventeenth and eighteenth centuries, he explained to Matthew's considerable surprise, Brazil had imported ten times as many slaves as the United States. When slavery was abolished at the end of the nineteenth century the free slaves, with few rights and no niche in the wider society, had created their own communities on the steep hillsides that the more affluent inhabitants of the city would have regarded as unsuitable for human habitation. In more recent times the mass migration of the poor from rural areas to the urban centres in search of work and a better standard of living had resulted in an explosion in the growth of these shanty towns to the point where a fifth of the population of Rio now lived in the *favelas*.

'Of course, the thing that gets the attention of the media,' Lucas told him in his perfect English as they finished their meal, 'is the drug trafficking. And it's undeniable that it is a part of life in the *favelas*. Corruption and violence are an ever-present danger. And too many of our young people get sucked into the drugs trade with the promise of easy money. But that's not the whole truth. Not by any means. Government agencies and other organisations are investing in development to improve the standard of living. Some of the larger banks are opening branches and setting up automatic teller machines. The police and social services have been working together in what's called *pacification* to reclaim whole areas from the control of the drug cartels. But the greatest force for good, in my opinion, doesn't come out of what government or big business is doing. From the Catholic Brotherhoods who worked among the slaves in the eighteenth century to the rapidly growing evangelical Christian denominations today, the Church, though not without its failings, has generally been a force for good. And the energy and resourcefulness of individuals and volunteer groups continue to have a transformative impact on life in the *favelas*.'

Lucas paused as his wife served them with small white cups of *cafezinho*. The bitter black coffee drew a gasp from Matthew and brought a smile to the face of his host.

'I suspect from your reaction, Mr Gold, that you're more of a tea drinker than a coffee connoisseur. Our strong Brazilian coffee is taking you by surprise.'

Matthew agreed that tea was indeed his customary beverage, but insisted, not entirely truthfully, that he was appreciating the opportunity to savour the taste and aroma of what his host assured him was the world's finest arabica coffee.

'I think that tomorrow, Mr Gold,' Lucas said as he showed Matthew to the guest bedroom, 'when I take you around our town and when you see what you've come all this way to see, you'll be gasping in surprise at much more than our national drink. And don't worry, I'll make sure that we find you some of your favourite tea.'

The next morning, when Matthew joined his hosts for *café de monhã*, he discovered that Lucas had already fulfilled his promise. While the others drank sweetened coffee from a glass with their toasted bread rolls and cake, he enjoyed the Earl Grey tea that Lucas had already succeeded in getting hold of for his guest from England. Breakfast didn't take long, and soon it was time to begin their tour. Walking and driving through the narrow alleys of the *favela* was an experience he would never forget.

'How d-d-do you know wh-where you're g-g-going?' he asked. 'D-d-don't you ever g-g-get lllost?'

'Well, it can get a little confusing, Mr Gold, even when you've lived here as long as I have.' Lucas pointed towards a chink of sunlight breaking through a gap in the buildings. 'But here's a tip, should you ever decide to come and live here. If you get lost in one of these alleys, look for the light and you'll find your way out.' Then he added with a chuckle, 'Come to think of it, that's not a bad rule for life…'

The longer the morning went on, the more amazed Matthew became by life in the *favela*. The houses had obviously not been constructed to any formalised legal building code; but somehow they stayed upright. The overhead cables, slung above his head and wrapped around tall poles like untidy tangles of thick black yarn, left him in no doubt that electricity had been installed piecemeal; but somehow it worked. They walked down streets where sewage ran in channels between the houses; but somehow people took a pride in their homes. They passed through a doorway set at a crazy angle; but somehow on the other side there was a functioning classroom occupied by eager children being taught by a smiling and enthusiastic teacher. Compared with his life and everything he possessed, the people he could see had very little; but somehow they seemed no less happy than his well-to-do neighbours back in Wilmound.

On and on it went – surprise after surprise – until at precisely twelve o'clock it was time, as Lucas had expressed it the previous evening, for Matthew to see what he'd come all this way to see. They were standing in front of a church, but their eyes were drawn to a single-storey square box of a building to the side that stood out from everything around it. The wall they were facing was painted in bold, wide yellow and green diagonal stripes broken only by a bright red door with a gleaming chrome doorbell. Lucas was about to press the bell when the door was opened by a slightly built woman whose white hair retained a reddish tinge and whose fair complexion contrasted with the darker skin tones they had seen around them all that morning.

'You got here safely, then, Matthew. Welcome. And you, too, Lucas.'

Elsie Ratcliffe's face was beaming as she greeted her visitors and led them along a corridor into a cramped office with barely room for the three of them to sit down. Matthew couldn't help but notice that she seemed, if anything, even more animated than on their only previous meeting. She'd been delighted when he'd got in touch with her a couple of months after their unexpected encounter at Sam Andrews' funeral to say that he'd like to see something of the work she did in some of the world's most deprived communities. He'd looked at her card lying on his desk numerous times since they'd met, but he'd always found an excuse for not getting in touch. But in the end, the niggling fear that he might follow his grandmother in leaving it too late to do what he knew he should do overcame his reticence. He'd surprised himself by picking up the phone and calling her rather than emailing. She'd recognised his voice immediately, of course, and didn't seem surprised that he'd called.

'I've been half-expecting you'd call after our chance meeting,' she said cheerfully, before adding, 'What took you so long?'

There was something about the inflection of her voice as she said the word 'chance' that made him think she thought their meeting was more than mere happenstance. As a writer of detective mysteries, he knew all about the importance of seemingly random events that turned out to be more significant than anyone first imagined. It was a little unsettling, however, to think that the same thing might hold true in real life. He let her remark pass without comment and tried not to think about it more than he could help.

He glanced at his watch after he'd put the receiver down at the end of that first phone call and was amazed to see that their conversation had lasted for half an hour. Half an hour in which he hadn't once got as embarrassed or as tongue-tied as he normally did on the phone. After that they'd called each other with increasing regularity until it became an almost weekly occurrence and the phone calls became face-to-face conversations thanks to the internet and webcams. Twice they'd even planned to meet up and spend a day together, only to have their plans spoiled on both occasions by the addition of last-minute engagements to Elsie's calendar. Now, almost a year after Sam's funeral in Manchester, they were meeting for only the second time as adults in a tiny room in a community clinic in a *favela* in Rio de Janeiro on a warm and sunny day in August. It had been many years since Matthew had broken into spontaneous laughter, but the improbability of the moment made him do exactly that. And Lucas and Elsie, seeing his expression and sensing his incredulity, shared in his amusement.

They sat talking together for a few minutes while cups of *cafezinho* were brought, which Elsie and Lucas received gratefully and drank with obvious pleasure. Matthew politely declined. Acquiring a taste for strong coffee, he reflected ruefully, was definitely something he *had* left too late. He waited patiently until Elsie, invigorated by her intake of caffeine, was ready to show them the work of the clinic.

'Come on, you two,' she said, finishing her last mouthful and banging her cup down on the table. 'We can't sit here all day. It's time for me to introduce you to some of the nicest people you'll ever meet.'

She led them into a much larger space, a waiting room that was crowded with mothers and children ranging from babies less than a year old to boys and girls whom Matthew judged to be around ten or eleven. Despite the differences in their ages, they all had one thing in common. Every child in the room had been born with a cleft lip or cleft palate. He could see that some were still waiting for surgery while others were in the early stages of recovery and healing following the procedure to correct the birth defect. It was a sight that brought tears to his eyes and a surge of rage that shocked him by its ferocity. It seemed so unfair that life had dealt these kids such a difficult hand. Growing up in a *favela* would have challenges enough without having to cope with the kind of facial disfigurements he saw all around him. It was only when the first rush of anger subsided that it occurred to him that he didn't normally feel such a sense of injustice about the handicaps that others had to deal with. There were, he acknowledged to himself, many people who carried heavier burdens than his. And there was, he realised, something changing in his attitude to life.

He stood to one side and listened as Lucas and Elsie moved around the room chatting briefly in Portuguese to both mothers and children. He couldn't understand what they were saying, but there was something he could tell instantly from the rhythm of their speech and the tone of their voices, something that would have been clear to any visitor who stepped into this room. If the sight of so much disfigurement was one that could induce anger and despair in anyone with a sense of fairness, the sound of so much hopefulness and gratitude was unmistakable and couldn't fail to bring pleasure to anyone with a modicum of humanity. The question these women would have asked from the moment they first saw and held their babies must surely have been: 'Why has this happened?' Even if they'd found an answer, Matthew reflected, it would have done little to ease their pain. But that question would have been quickly superseded by one that was much more pressing: 'What can be done to make this better?' And what he was hearing was the happiness and relief that come to people who haven't discovered an explanation for life's unfairness but who have been given an expectation that there is help and there is hope.

It was five o'clock in the evening before Matthew stepped through the door of the clinic with Lucas and back into the alleyway. He tried to reorientate himself to the world of the *favela* he'd left just a few hours before, blinking in the evening sunshine and jumping back as a motorbike roared past at breakneck speed. He felt as if he'd just emerged from a portal that had allowed him access to a parallel universe in which the process of learning was speeded up and in which one experience followed another so rapidly that there was a constant danger of sensory overload. For a man who'd spent so much time alone, protecting himself from the world for so many years, it would take some time to process all he'd seen and heard in one afternoon.

That evening Elsie joined them for dinner in the garden of Lucas' house. While they chatted, alternating easily between English and Portuguese, Matthew sat quietly, saying little and barely hearing what they were saying. As soon as the meal was over, he excused himself and went to his room. He lay on the bed with his eyes closed, going over the events of the day. They'd gone from the waiting room into a series of consultations with some of the mothers, explaining to them what would be involved in surgery and how they could best care for their child in the interim. That had been followed by a meeting with a group of doctors with whom Elsie had shared her expertise in cleft surgery. Trying to listen attentively to Lucas' whispered running translation of what was being said was tiring in itself and made him want to close his eyes and sleep for twenty minutes. But none of that compared to what followed. Dressed in scrubs to match the medical team and seated on a stool at a safe distance from the operating table, he'd watched with a mixture of fascination and squeamishness while a very young-looking doctor performed a cleft repair on a little girl just nine months old. Under Elsie's practised eye, the trainee surgeon had carefully connected the muscles of the soft palate and rearranged the tissues to close the cleft. His hands were preternaturally still and only the beads of sweat that appeared on his forehead betrayed the intense concentration the procedure demanded of him.

It had been the most exhilarating and exhausting day of Matthew's life. But what stood out above everything else and what would stay with him for the rest of his life would be the sights and sounds of the waiting room. In the faces of those disfigured children he'd been confronted again by the mystery of pain and suffering and injustice. But in the longing eyes and anxious voices of their mothers, in the matter-of-fact way in which Elsie had moved round the room and chatted to them offering help and hope, he thought he'd caught a glimpse of something else. He reached into his suitcase and unzipped the compartment where he kept his passport and travel documents. He fumbled for a moment until he found the letter he'd looked at so many times during the past year and that he'd been careful to bring with him on this trip. He read Sam's tiny handwriting again:

But there is a greater mystery – one that I believe is deeper and stronger than the mystery of evil and suffering. And that deeper mystery is this: when someone willingly takes the pain and suffering around them upon themselves, refuses to be beaten or contaminated by it, a wonderful and unexpected transformation takes place. Healing appears where there is hurt, beauty appears where there is ugliness, joy appears where there is misery, forgiveness appears where there is bitterness, love appears where there is hate, good appears where there is evil.

In the morning he would tell Lucas and Elsie that the trip had been well worthwhile and that he really had seen what he'd come all this way to see.

chapter 32

2019

The waiting area in the Oncology Unit of Wilmound Private Hospital, with its cream leather armchairs, stylish wall art and soothing background music had been thoughtfully designed and sensitively decorated to provide an oasis of calm for patients who might be about to hear news that would be difficult for them to receive. The only two people sitting there on Monday 11th March remarked to each other that it was in complete contrast to the noisy and crowded waiting room of the clinic in the Brazilian *favela* they had both visited just six months earlier. The woman also commented to her male companion that, pleasant as their surroundings were, it probably wasn't the place where he would have chosen to be on his seventy-second birthday. He was about to respond to that comment when a third person came into the room.

'Mr Gold.' The young nurse smiled reassuringly as she spoke. 'Mr Chakrabarti will see you now.'

Matthew stood up and slowly followed her, with the help of Elsie Ratcliffe who took his arm and walked alongside him.

'D-D-Do you mmmind if mmy...' he started to ask as they reached the door of the consultant's office.

'Of course not, of course not,' Mr Chakrabarti replied warmly, as he pointed them to a couple of chairs in front of his desk. 'Your wife must join us. She should hear what I have to say.'

'Oh, I'm not Mr Gold's wife.' Elsie quickly corrected his error. 'Just a very old friend who's come to give some moral support. And I'm a doctor, so maybe I can help answer any questions that come to mind for my friend over the next few days.'

The consultant shook hands with them both before sitting down and running his right hand slowly across the file that was lying on his desk. He hesitated for a moment, and looked carefully at Matthew, as if trying to gauge the likely reaction of his patient to what he was about to hear. He pushed the file to the side, clasped his hands in front of him and began to speak in a quiet but clear voice.

'Now, Mr Gold. Tell me, please. How honest would you like me to be?'

Matthew nodded knowingly at Elsie. He'd told her on the way to the hospital that he was sure he wasn't about to be given good news. Turning back to face the consultant, he took some slow, deep breaths.

'I'd b-b-be g-g-grateful if you'd be comp-comp-completely honest, p-please.'

Elsie reached across and took hold of his hand. Matthew sat as still as he could and tried to compose himself. Mr

Chakrabarti pulled his chair a little closer to his desk and reached for the file again.

'Thank you. That makes this conversation a little easier for both of us. Let me tell you exactly where we are and what we can and cannot do. All the scans and tests we've done over the last few weeks confirm beyond any doubt that you have stage 4 pancreatic cancer. I can go through all these reports in detail if you want me to do that. But the bottom line is that the cancer is very aggressive and very far advanced. The prognosis is not good. Your condition is terminal, Mr Gold. We can help with palliative care and with medication that will give you some ease from your pain and discomfort. But there is no cure that we can offer. The cancer has already spread into your lungs and your bones. That's why you've been having so much pain and such difficulty with your breathing in the last few months.'

Matthew felt Elsie gently squeeze his hand. There was only one question he wanted to ask.

'I appre-appreciate you b-being so truthful. How lllong d-d-do I have?'

'That's always difficult to say. Sometimes patients surprise us and live far longer than we think. We doctors certainly don't know everything. But given your condition and the extent to which the cancer has metastasised, probably no more than two or three months, possibly even just a few weeks. I'm sorry, but it's impossible to be more precise than that. If you need to put your affairs in order, it's best not to delay. And we can help you sort out hospice care, of course.'

Matthew was about to explain that while he appreciated the offer of hospice care, he was determined to spend his last days at home. But before he could get the words out, Elsie had released her grip on his hand and spoken for him.

'Thank you, Mr Chakrabarti, but I'm well enough acquainted with this man by now to know that he won't want to go into residential hospice care, excellent though that would be. We both had a fair idea of what you would tell us today. I've already cancelled all my appointments for the foreseeable future. He has a large house with room for a resident nurse who, in this case, will be me.'

She winked at Matthew and took hold of his hand again as Mr Chakrabarti looked on.

'You see, Mr Chakrabarti,' Elsie added, 'it's taken me sixty years to catch up with this man since the day I saw him standing soaked to the skin in the rain on the edge of a muddy football field looking like he needed somebody to take care of him. I let him get away then. But not this time. This is my opportunity to look after him.'

They left the consultant's office and walked arm in arm back to the car park in silence. Matthew's overwhelming emotion was one of relief that the weeks of uncertainty were over. He'd begun to feel tired and unwell shortly after returning from his week in Rio. At first, he'd assumed that it was just the after-effects of travel or the result of a bug he must have picked up in the crowded conditions of the *favela*. It was only after he'd described how he was feeling to Elsie in a phone conversation that, at her insistence, he'd gone to see his doctor, who had immediately referred him to the hospital. The reaction of the specialist he'd seen then, the number of tests he'd gone through, and his own awareness of how increasingly unwell he was feeling left him in little doubt that he was facing a serious illness. Now he knew the truth and it was time, as he'd just been advised, to 'put his affairs in order'. But as he began to think about it, he replaced that phrase with another that more accurately described what he had to do. He wouldn't just put things in order. *He'd put them right.*

In just over a week, he'd drawn up his will, something he'd never got round to doing, despite the constant prompting of his solicitor. He left his money to a number of good causes, but primarily to the charity that Elsie worked with and to one that conducted research into the causes and treatment of stammering. He also set up The Monty Silver Foundation, to be administered by someone Elsie would appoint, that would use any future income from his literary estate to make grants to promising young writers. He wanted to leave a substantial amount of money to Elsie in gratitude for her care in his last days, had she not threatened to leave him to look after himself if he did such a thing.

'I'm comfortably off,' she insisted. 'And what would I do with that amount of money? I'd only waste it on riotous living and buying the most expensive coffee money can buy. I'd end up being so hyperactive that I'd drive everybody crazy.'

As the days passed, he grew steadily weaker, his breathing more laboured, and the pain became gradually more intense. But with the drug regime that had been prescribed and Elsie's attentive care, the discomfort did not become unbearable. Sleep was fitful and frequently involved vivid encounters with people who'd figured prominently in his past. He rode again on Grampa's shoulders to Verricchia's Ice Cream Parlour; he sat at his desk in Mrs Evans' class, safe from the unwanted attentions of Danny Johnstone; he ate breakfast at Ma Smith's house listening to The Beatles on the radio; he perched on the edge of the table at Bellmill Academy, dangling his legs with Mr McFadyen; he walked through Kelvingrove Park in the sunshine on his way to the university; he ate lunch in expensive restaurants with Julian and Emmeline Barrington-Williams; he drank Earl Grey tea with Sam Andrews in The Sanctuary Tearoom; he even stood in the old scullery at 121 Pit Road talking happily with his grandmother. In his more lucid waking hours, he reasoned that these seeming visitations were somewhere between dreams and hallucinations brought on by the effects of the medication. He was not ungrateful for them. He received them as a gift, a final opportunity to visit his past before his conscious memory would shut down and darkness would close in.

And they had an additional benefit for which he was, if anything, even more grateful. The more these visions of the past occurred, the less room there was for his recurring nightmare of the scattered manuscript and the three missing pages. It had figured in his dreams only once since he'd received the diagnosis of stage 4 pancreatic cancer. But there was one significant difference. This time in his dream, he'd quickly put the manuscript back in order and he'd been able to complete those final pages, apart from a closing paragraph. And rather than the panic that had always broken his sleep previously, he'd woken with a quiet sense that it wasn't quite time for him to complete the manuscript and that he'd know what to write in those concluding sentences when the moment came.

He was sitting one afternoon looking out of the window at the garden when Elsie asked him if there was anything he wanted. He looked at her with a slightly embarrassed expression before he told her what had been in his mind for several days.

'You know, there is sssomething. It mmmight sound a b-b-bit silly, but I wwwant to have a p-p-party. I'm ssseventy-two, I haven't g-g-got lllong to live and I think it's t-t-time for mmme to throw a p-p-party – b-before it's too lllate.'

He could see the look of surprise on Elsie's face, and he quickly assured her that this was neither an attempt at black humour, a way of coping with his impending death, nor the result of confusion brought on by the medication. He was thinking clearly and he meant exactly what he said. *He wanted to throw a party in his garden. A proper party.* A party with no expense spared. A party with printed personalised invitations. A party with live music. A party with generous helpings of good food. A party for his neighbours. A party for anyone with whom he'd had contact who might be able and willing to come.

Only someone with Elsie's energy and enthusiasm for life would have contemplated taking on such a seemingly impossible task. But after a hectic few days of frenetic activity on her part, countless phone calls, and five separate face-to-face meetings with the representative from the event organising company they'd been able to hire at short notice, the invitations had gone out – most of them by email, some by the postal service, and a few even hand-delivered by Elsie herself – to a party on Easter

Saturday in the garden of Mr Matthew Gold's home at Number 7, The Rookery, Wilmound.

At three o'clock in the afternoon of Good Friday, as the bells solemnly tolled thirty-three times in the nearby church, Matthew's condition appeared to suddenly worsen. Elsie began to think that the excitement had proved too much for him and to regret that she'd allowed herself to be persuaded that organising a celebration was a good idea. By the evening, however, he had rallied slightly and she could detect in him a fierce determination to host the one and only party of his life. She checked on him almost every hour during the night, fearing the worst each time she looked into his bedroom. But he woke early in the morning, appearing to have found a new lease of life, and determined to check with her repeatedly that everything was ready for when their guests would arrive.

At two o'clock on Easter Saturday, under clear blue skies and a bright warm sun, the guests began to arrive. At first it was just a trickle, and Elsie wondered again if they'd made a mistake. But within half an hour nearly 400 people were spread across every corner of the garden at Number 7, The Rookery. None of them had been sure what to expect and every one of them had been taken aback by the scene that greeted them. Streams of colourful bunting stretched from tree to tree. There was a large marquee filled with tables draped in dazzling white cloths and bearing an array of food catering for every possible taste. At the end of the garden furthest from the house, a stage had been erected with two impressive-looking banks of speakers. And at precisely 2.30 The SkaReds Band mounted the stage and launched into their set of infectiously rhythmic songs.

Those who were old enough and who'd been hip enough in their youth, recognised them immediately as the Ska hits of the 1980s, and those who were still fit enough began to dance. The fifty or so children present gravitated to the carousel and the bouncy castle that had been set up alongside a bright red van from which large ice creams would be freely distributed later in the afternoon.

Matthew himself sat in a wickerwork chair, propped up with cushions to support his painful back, and did his best to greet each guest in turn as they arrived. He was pleased and surprised that many more of his neighbours had turned up than he could have hoped for, particularly considering that he'd given them such short notice of the event and that he'd kept them at such a distance for such a long time. Others had travelled from further afield. Marco and Julia Verricchia had driven from Bellmill to meet, for only the second time, the man who'd been a patron of their Ice Cream Parlour as a child. The owner of The Sanctuary Tearoom had closed her business for the afternoon so that she and the entire staff could attend and honour one of their regulars. Elsie's son had left his partner to look after his market stall and had taken the morning train from London to give his mother a hand and see who this man was who'd come to mean so much to her in the last few months. And Ian Andrews arrived with his son, Finn, who shook hands very formally with Matthew, took a deep breath as he'd been taught by his grandfather, said very slowly, 'Hello, Mmmr Gold. It's nnnice to mmmeet you again,' and then ran off in the direction of the bouncy castle. Matthew noticed that the boy's stammer had improved since they'd last met more than two years before and it pleased him to think of the difference that would make to his life.

Later in the afternoon, when The SkaReds Band had completed their set and food had been served, everyone gathered in front of the stage as Finn Andrews and twenty of his classmates, all of whom had been marched somewhat reluctantly from the bouncy castle and were now dressed in their school uniforms, mounted the steps to the platform. They were the members of the choir Matthew had heard singing in the church next to The Sanctuary Tearoom on the day he'd first met Sam Andrews, and he'd instructed Elsie that whatever else did or didn't happen at his party, she must make sure that they would be there. They sang three lively songs from their repertoire to enthusiastic applause from the audience before their teacher sounded a long note on a tuning pipe. There was a moment's silence before Finn's solo voice began to sing very softly and without any accompaniment:

By cool Siloam's shady rill
How fair the lily grows!
How sweet the breath, beneath the hill,
Of Sharon's dewy rose!

The other children picked up a second verse of the old hymn:

By cool Siloam's shady rill
The lily must decay;
The rose that blooms beneath the hill
Must shortly fade away.

One of the girls in the choir then played through the simple melody on her flute before they all sang the first verse again. And when they had finished there was no applause. Only the sound of birdsong and the rustling of leaves in the warm breeze.

When the children had filed slowly and quietly off the stage, Elsie introduced Scott Handone, who'd played the title role in the television adaptation of the *Monty Silver Mysteries*. Mr Handone, she explained, had agreed to read some words that their host had prepared and would have spoken himself had he felt strong enough. People began to clap as the well-known actor came to the mic, but he immediately halted their applause with a wave of his hand and indicated towards Matthew, who was sitting in the front row looking up at him.

'Ladies and gentlemen, it has been my privilege to deliver some of Mr Gold's best lines on your television screens. But today is a much greater privilege even than that was. When I played the role of the slick-talking Monty Silver, I spoke words that I'd learned from a script. Today I have memorised words that Matthew Gold has written that I know come straight from his heart. Take a moment to be still and prepare *your* heart to hear and receive what he has to say to us.'

He cleared his throat, smiled at Matthew, and began to speak.

There are only a few words I want to say to you this afternoon. They are words we all need to say to each other much more than we do. They are certainly words that I wish I'd said a lot earlier and a lot more often in my life.

I want to say thank you. Thank you to all of you for accepting my invitation. And thank you to everyone who has shown me kindness throughout my life, but especially in recent years. Your generosity means so much to me.

I want to say sorry. Sorry to so many people who are not here today. Sorry to my neighbours from whom I shut myself away for too long. Sorry to the staff of The Sanctuary Tearoom to whom my daily silence must have seemed aloof and ungrateful. Sorry for the fact that, faced with the mystery of pain and suffering, I retreated from life. Sorry that what I thought was independence and self-sufficiency was really just fear and selfishness.

I want to say please. Please forgive me for the hurt I have caused to so many people and to some of you here today. And please accept this party as a gift from me. It's taken me too long to learn the joy and release of giving.

Finally, I want to say goodbye. I know that I don't have many days left to live and I'm a little sad that I have to leave this world a few years earlier than I might have wished. I *am* sad, but I am not at all unhappy. Indeed, these recent years have been the happiest of my life. The mystery of pain and hurt touches all of us some time in our lives. But on my seventieth birthday just over two years ago, a wise and good man introduced me to a mystery beyond the mystery. He gave me some words that I have committed to memory, and I share them with you now:

But there is a greater mystery – one that I believe is deeper and stronger than the mystery of evil and suffering. And that deeper mystery is this: when someone willingly takes the pain and suffering around them upon themselves, refuses to be beaten or contaminated by it, a wonderful and unexpected transformation takes place. Healing appears where there is hurt, beauty appears where there is ugliness, joy appears where there is misery, forgiveness appears where there is bitterness, love appears where there is hate, good appears where there is evil.

The man of whom I've just told you, the man who gave me those words, faced death with a willingness to risk everything on their truth. I'm not quite so brave as he was and I'm maybe a little less certain than he was, but I'm determined to take the same risk that he did.

There's just one more thing to say. This afternoon must not end with solemn words from me but with another hour of music and dancing. This is a party, not a wake! Please welcome The SkaReds Band back to the stage. And let the dancing begin.

Scott Handone walked from the mic and the members of The SkaReds Band came back onto the stage and picked up their instruments. For almost a minute no one in the crowd moved. But as soon as the opening riff sounded from the lead guitar, the garden of Number 7, The Rookery, became a sea of bodies moving with joyous abandon to the rhythm of the music. And as the dance went on, two people walked slowly arm in arm, almost unnoticed by their guests, around the edge of the garden and into the house.

They sat together by an open window in the kitchen for a while, drinking tea and listening as the festivities continued unabated outside.

'It's been an exhausting day,' Elsie said, reaching over and closing the window. 'I think it's time for some quietness now.'

'Yes. Thank you, Elsie,' Matthew replied. 'It's all b-b-been worthwhile. We've had a p-p-party and I was able to g-g-go.'

She thought she could see a look of longing in his eyes and she wondered if he'd wanted to stay a little longer in the garden.

'Do you want to go back out and join them again for a while?' she asked.

He shook his head and gave a tired smile. Then he took some deep breaths and spoke very slowly.

'Oh no. That's enough partying. Now I've got some things I still have to sort out. There's a right time to leave the party and get ready to go home.'

Also by Chick Yuill:

When the caretaker of St Peter's finds that the church has been broken into early on the Saturday morning after Christmas and that the elderly intruder is still in the building and kneeling at the communion rail, no one is quite sure what to do.

But the confusion caused by the sudden arrival of this unexpected visitor is as nothing compared to the impact of his continuing presence on the church and the town. As his identity becomes clear and his story unfolds, long-hidden truths emerge, and life in Penford can never be quite the same again…

Instant Apostle, 2018, ISBN 978-1-909728-87-5

Where can a man find grace when he no longer believes? Ray Young has been married for almost thirty years. But his once vibrant faith, like his marriage, is steadily fading, and relations with his only son Ollie are increasingly strained. Facing this looming crisis of faith, Ray begins an affair, only for Ollie to discover his father's infidelity. Confronted by his actions, Ray has one chance to rescue the life that is crumbling around him. But when tragedy strikes, it seems all hope of redemption is gone…

Instant Apostle, 2018, ISBN 978-1-909728-65-3